D0443174

3 0600 00447 1885

Pierre Clitandre

Cathedral
of the
August Heat

translated by Bridget Jones

readers international

The title of this work in French is *Cathédrale du mois d'août,* first published in 1982 in Paris by Editions Syros.

Copyright © Editions Syros 1982

First published in English by Readers International Inc., London and New York, whose editorial branch is at 8 Strathray Gardens, London NW3 4NY England. US/Canadian inquiries to Subscriber Service Department, P.O. Box 959, Columbia Louisiana 71418-0959 USA.

The editors and translator gratefully acknowledge the assistance of Valerie Bloom and Marie-José Nzengou-Tayo, among others, in the preparation of this book.

Cover Art: Haitian mural
Design by Jan Brychta
Typesetting by Grassroots Typeset, London NW6
Printed and Bound in Great Britain by Richard Clay Ltd, Bungay, Suffolk

ISBN 0-930523-30-X Hardcover
ISBN 0-930523-31-8 Paperback

To Violette Jean-Gilles Clitandre,
without whom my memory would not be
filled with dreams and miracles...
and to my father, who disappeared in the custody
of the Tontons Macoutes when going to visit a friend,
July 16, 1982

PART ONE

Vèvè for Erzulie

Vèvè, or mystical sign in the voodoo religion, for *Erzulie*, the goddess of love, divinity of dreams and muse of beauty.

Endlessly flashing their chrome, dancing their way down the too-narrow avenue went the *tap-taps*, the poor men's buses painted with pious images, weaving between the crowds of a town no bigger than the span of your hand.

Our Lady of August went by, creaking like an old hand-cart, trailing a sad stink of grease, bad breath and sweat.

— What time, *m'sieu?*

— Eleven o'clock.

— Holy Virgin, Mother of Miracles!...

The bus rolled on, crammed with unshaven faces, hard-veined hands, hats rammed down on brows furrowed with pain, where the flecks of dried sweat were pale as the earth on the salt flats. Some wore heavy shoes with thick soles, heavier hearted still with the dust or mud of several days. In the dense air inside, between the two rows of passengers looking bad-tempered and weary, up into their dried-up faces broken and bruised by heat and fatigue floated the acrid smell of a spent cigarette butt, which joined with the choking fumes from the backside of their beat-up transport—enough to hold off a silver Mercedes with an itchy horn that was signalling to the traffic cop on the corner.

The bus jolted on, creaking from every joint of its patch-up of planks, zinc sheets, iron, parcels and people; the bodywork nearly reached down to touch the asphalt strip, and though the colours had faded through bad weather and big dirty hands, you could still read some naive lettering:

Saint Rose of Lima, Watch over your children...

or:

The Lord shall fight for you, and ye shall hold your peace... (Exodus 14:14).

Squeezed tight in their seats, the passengers felt the cramp crawl up their calves like a million red ants marching to attack, while heavy trickles of sweat ran down their backs like a lick from a cow's tongue.

Again and again the old bus rocked the two lines of passengers back and forth, welded into one or suddenly unshackled by the shock of a screeching brake. The sun beat down on the asphalt. No one signalled it to stop as it groaned and juddered and backfired along the road like a soul in torment. You don't hitch a ride with death. No one could read the number plate pasted over with a thick layer of dried mud and the windscreen, crazed in some accident, had inspired a decorative hand to trace the pattern of cracks into a marvellous spider's web like a great golden sun bursting over the glass.

That engine not going so good. And is only last week I pay out twenty dollar for a grease and check. Mechanic no come no better than shoemaker. Just take the cash you work so hard for in the sun. The road no good to me you know. Good luck left me long time.

Nothing but bad luck a-ride me back: fine to pay, them threaten me with jail, the cop with him whistle and you want to smash-up him ugly face, red light stop you with only one fare on the bus, gas to buy, and the man cuss you off if you don't stop at him own front door...Some of them want you to set them down on the bed itself!

Me, is only one old mattress me have. Raphael wet it up plenty since him come from the hospital. I still spread it out

2

in the sun to get rid of the bugs and stink. Can't remember when I did buy it and I don't have no woman again to lie down there. Madeleine use to cook the corn nice; she was a good piece of woman, but she was a whore. When she left, me table and me chairs, even me Italian shoes left with her. And is me have to feed the boy, and buy him the boots and the books him need for school.

And is struggle I struggle! If a screw or a nail go try drop out of the truck body, must catch them in time; that old radiator can't last much longer. Holy Virgin, just must hold up! Me holding on to it, that's for sure. Is an old crock, a skinned rat done many a mile. But, Lord, how I long for its health and strength. Need new tyres. But where the money coming from?...Shit! You hear the noise those con rod making!... Should o' stop, turn everybody off, check why the blasted con rod them complaining so.... But so many 50 centime fares, them will just melt way and gone you know! And I can't stop on the corner with the cop looking out for me....

Alright, pass me out! You blasted horn getting on me nerves! Pass me out if me crate smell like ram-goat! Right on!.... See them. See them pick up speed in them luxury limousine!...

Why you can't press the bell button! If that glass break, you going pay me!... What you say? I not doing the job properly? Eight years I been on the road. Is not a whore like you going to tell me my business...I work the route. If one of you in too much hurry, get off and let me get on with the job! And another thing, no other bus will take fish-market woman with oonu nastiness!...you mothers!...

Up tight, all sweaty, he took a cigarette out of his pocket and lit it. That smell of engine fumes and cigarette stubs clung to the old bus like its own scent. No ram-goat stink, just the day after day smell of John, who gets up every morning at four o'clock, whistles while he washes the old Ford, and comes back at night soaked in sweat, with a face like a funeral.

He had loved Madeleine when he saw her fornicating with the white man who smelt of tobacco. It had caught him full in the face in the doorway, that tobacco smell, as he was slipping into the woman's room to smell the mint. Holding his nose, he edged silently into the little blue-painted room with a light bulb in the ceiling which shone down on the bare red buttocks of the customer, sizzling with sweat like fat on the fire. Madeleine caught his eye but never stopped the soft serpent sound that hissed between her clenched teeth and sent electric shocks into the soft mass of flesh grunting on her like a pig.

And John's rod had arisen.

For the very first time since the day when trouble and debts and liquor began to eat away his sleep. Every time he tried to make love, his beast just hung down like the flap on a turkey's bill. He had brewed potions and essences of cow dung, duck egg, root of stand-up *liana*, bark of *hol'up-mi-seed*, green herbs, and all kinds of things, hoping to get back his nature. Nothing helped. Then he understood that he had been tied up by a spell, and he consulted the *obeah*-man. He took his advice and his remedies, reciting prayers to St. James the Great. Nothing helped. And so, since then, he believed he was limbless for life, and he grieved.

Women mocked him after they had tried a night with him on that pissy mattress of his and found him as hard to love as a *tonton-macoute*. And John felt shame, until the night when it came to his mind to spend the ten dollars at the bottom of his pocket in a sad café. And the mint-scented woman caught his eye, the one who was so good at dancing the *guaracha* and the *bolero*.

After that, the café became his favourite place to pass the time. He made friends with the manageress, an old lady sheathed all over in cheap gold, heavy red painted on her bony cheeks, heavy green on her eyelids, wrinkled by so many weary times and sleepless nights spent between the cash till and the rum and the music howling out from her old-time sound system: a face that came to you from another age. Sometimes there behind her counter she would tell him stories of crazy customers, or memories of time past, like that couple from the days of the opening of the Bicentenary Exhibition, who won a nice bit of money by dancing nonstop for eight days to the tune of

Carolina Aca-o
Me dance de congo till me body da ache
Carolina Aca-o
Small ear black man enragé

Those were the days of panama hats, white suits and stiletto heels. Those days you could pay five gourdes to see amazing hermaphrodites and turtles with young ladies' heads.

One night the mint-scented woman came up to him as he leaned on the counter. When he looked into her heavy wasting eyes, he could see as many pale gleams as on the wooden café floor, polished by the groggy steps of drunken Yankee sailors, and tight-pant youths who looked like fancy-boys, and the young men with the look of revolt, adventure and escape.

—Hi there, man, *como está?*

—*Muy bien*! Trying to keep going. That's how it stay.

He breathed in the scent of mint that came from between her flat breasts and under her arms. And breathing in her heady perfume, it came to him that he hadn't bathed, because for two days the pipe at the fountain had stopped giving cold water, and he fretted at his smell of engine fumes, salt and ram-goat.

Nothing much developed in the way of chat. Keeping his problem to himself, he curled up inwardly like a dog hanging his tail at the sight of death. A hunted beast. And she for her part couldn't understand why he cotched his rum bottle so tight between his legs each time she met his eyes, as she paused for breath in the arms of some tame customer.

5

So it was until that night when he trembled all over like a peeping pickney, and saw the backside of the white man who smelled of tobacco, and heard that hissing breath of Madeleine.

And in one mad rage, he lifted up that red naked body light as a feather, swung it up in the air like a cock to the slaughter. And the man just coming to come sprayed his seed everywhere like a tap burst open: from the bed to the ceiling, on the floor, on the wall, on the almanacs, the powder pots, the vials of scents and the flask of mint-water, on the print of the Virgin and even on the woman's face....

John flung himself down on her full of fire and took her.

The white man with the tobacco smell sneaked on his pants, put on his black shirt, picked up from the table his big dark-bound book, slipped it under his left arm and ran out of the room, like he couldn't believe he was still alive after facing this wild male with eyes on fire.

It was an old priest. Some time later they had to make him give up the cloth, he made so much scandal with that hot tail of his.

Three days John and Madeleine spent coiled together, moving to the tune of the serpent's hiss that whispered from their closed teeth. And like a voice from beyond the grave came the song the old madam at the bar was still humming away:

Carolina Aca-o
Small ear black man enragé...

6

The bus creaked and whined along the ribbon of grey asphalt. It was hot as an oven. And every here and there the sun blazed back like metal. John wiped his face and forehead with the back of his hand. His other hand resting on the gear shift was clammy wet and trembled anxiously at times. Same down-hearted feeling looking at the little cashbox, in spite of the beaming face of Our-Lady-of-Perpetual-Help, Queen of Eternal Protection against the woes here below, pasted up with starch on the dusty windscreen beside the golden spider's web.

The cigarette butt burnt down to his lips. Smoking this Government brand hadn't lasted five minutes and the memory already gone. A fare stopped him, he pressed on the sagging brake pedal, collected the fifty centimes and threw them in the little till.... These automatic gestures, he repeated them day after day and his thick fingers smelt of the worn gourde coins, cigarette ash and engine oil.

That old Ford, from the very day he bought her from a man who was leaving for Nassau—with three thousand gourdes he'd won one Sunday in the lottery—from the moment he started the engine for the first time and heard the husky asthmatic sound that was to haunt him for years on end, she seemed a chronic invalid, afflicted with all those diseases: flu, plague, cholera, typhoid and blue fever, which were infecting the whole country and frightening away the people like a great flock of migrating birds.

His mind stayed wedded to the notion that in the machine's veins ran a whole complex of wasting illnesses inherited from the man leaving for Nassau. Could be a jinx. In no time at all John fixed up the bus with a bush bath of acacia leaves, *gungo* pea, lemon balm and wild sage to ward off bad luck.

He arranged for ten young voodoo sisters all in white to dance around the vehicle. Lit an everlasting candle in his little scented shrine. And on Christmas Eve, standing on a wicker chair, he emptied three bottles of cow's milk over his head while the bells were pealing out midnight from every church.

The bus was scrubbed down so vigorously—all the body work, the worn tyres, the rusty, dusty, springs, the stove-in seats, the lettering which didn't match the new owner's beliefs, the belly of the engine with all the bolt-on parts removed—that two days after this ritual bath, when John got a mechanic to come and start the engine, as he unscrewed the radiator cap such a strong spray of citronnella water and lemon balm gushed out that the man smelled sweet for a whole week.

As for John, he didn't want to take off for Nassau or any other island. Not that he was patriotic or averse to swelling that mass of men already running from plague, flu and blue fever by risking their luck with the bold, hardy boatmen. Though so many finished—boatmen and their strange cargoes—trussed up like pigs. No, he was worried about his son Raphael who'd just turned five, the child of his short-lived love affair with Madeleine. So he had decided to fight back against hunger and plague, be brave and valiant and break the evil spells. He would save the boy from the great curse, even though he had felt its hand upon him since that day he found his tail just dangling like a turkey's wattle.

One afternoon when a breakdown stopped him from working, John had gone a few steps from his home to see the bodies drowned in the sewer.

Rain had fallen for a full day without stopping and the sewage overflow had come down, carrying out toward the sea beds with broken springs, rusty metal sheets, planks from collapsed shacks and all kinds of other things while the people of the slum keened their woe. Next day, under a grudging zombie sun, the people found corpses of men, women and dogs blocking the mouth of the drain and floating on the filthy water. No one knew them. No one wept for them. Some among them wore extraordinary long shoes; others had no more than a ragged teat for a breast.

The Justice of the Peace was called, a gentleman in a tired grey suit, afraid that the mud would dirty his trousers and his shoes. He made a tally with the help of a long tree branch specially cut for the purpose—seven unidentified dead; then he left without a word.

Two days the people waited, but no one came to take away the dead. They began to rot, and the rotting gave off such an abominable stench as far as ten blocks of shacks, so that a new tally had to be made: on the roofs sixty dying pigeons, fifteen hens in yards, ten sows in their mire and five newborn babes in their blankets all stricken by a kind of paralysis, fallen victim to the fatal air of death.

Then the people in their panic ran down the lanes and the old passageways, their hair standing on end, crying:

— Smell the plague! Smell the plague!

Like rats they came from every hole. Some with picture magazines meant to paper the inside walls of their shacks, some with candle-rings, some with dry wood, some with matches; and a multitude went down towards the corpses in the drain and made a great bonfire upon them, chanting and clapping their hands:

— Plague go way!...Plague go way!...Plague go way!...

The sixty dead pigeons they hung out like laundry on a

line, till the feathers went with the wind and only the bones remained, powdering into dust, burnt by the tropical sun and eaten by red ants. The hens and the sows they cremated in the fire, and buried the babes in a common grave.

Without a single tear.

Thus did the people take revenge on the fearful nauseous smell of plague.

That night of revolt, incense was burned in every shack, and the scented vapour, mingling with the funeral pyre, rose up to the stars.

John spat out of the bus door onto the asphalt. A woman inside said:

— You make it half past eleven now, *m'sieu?*

— Twenty to twelve.

— But how long this driver been crawling along? I begin to feel a cramp in me belly. I set out this morning without a mouthful of coffee to push the wind off me chest.

— Nothing but a couple biscuit to eat a morning. Now the children... You have some of your own?...The pickney them spend the whole blessed day like that, them belly empty. I fret when they go all about the place, God knows where....

— That is true, me dear. Me had a child, a little boy four year old, a big truck crush him dead like a chicken. He couldn't understand town is hell. Him still believe it was country. All the *loa* spirit mount me head that day, one after another. *Papa Zaca* vex with me because I never warn him I was leaving the land. True it was there I grow up like the corn. But nothing no back there but dust and thorn. Thorn kill out the new shoot. The plant them did sick. Every day a next man left the land and gone out on the highway to stop the truck going to town. Everything rotten. The river come like a row of teeth. If you go back there now, all you would o' find would be zombies in the empty house them. *Papa Zaca* must can understand that. The man them strength left them for true.

— Is where you come from?

— Over by the Border. I try one time to cross over to the Dominican side; but it never work out.

— And you? Where you from?

— I can't remember at all.

The man had lost his memory. So tormented was he by hunger and the plague.

— I did think I was the only Christian to suffer from that hole in the middle of your head! Sometime I forget which alleyway lead to my box house. I have to ask some people passing by to help me find me hutch hide away in this graveyard. And yet six year I been living in the same place.

The memory sickness hadn't taken everything away. He still could remember exactly that April day when he sold a pig and a bull, won a hundred and two gourdes betting at the cockfight, and with his woman who wept and his children who jumped for joy, came to town.

— St. Rose of Lima protect you still, *m'sieu*. Your wife still able to bathe you head when you mind not easy, and rub you belly with castor oil when it swell up with gas. My man, him dead. Long time now him pass over. He promised to shower me with pesos and teach me the 'panish talk of the mulatto girls with mermaids' braids as soon as him come back. But him never come back. The last letter finish so strange: "We are organising..." Few months later I hear the news, they cut off him head on a sugar plantation and scraped up him bones with the dung.... So, me too, I take the road to town.

The woman bowed down her head and forgot the cramp in her empty belly.

The man with no memory offered her his cigarette. Since the chat inside the bus began he had an absent look as if he was trying to recall something. The story of the husband who lost his head woke him up with a shock.

— Beg pardon? Take this cigarette, me dear.

— Thank you, *m'sieu*! That will give me some ease.

And she inhaled deeply.

— A man who come back from Cuba, she went on, he tell me the story, tell me say, he had a neck thick like the cotton-tree trunk, break up the table when him talk, strong like a bull, and when the people hear him, them turn mad...

— Him blood did run hot.

— That was a black man didn't have big mouth just to say tenky massa!

— But, Jesus Lord, they kill Christian people like them pigs for slaughter!...

— ...Who say we Christian people? We are beast. Beast!...

— Men we must be, I know so... We have hand to nail and foot to walk when we don't have fifty centimes for the bus.

— Paws of a beast!...And he held out his stiffened arms.

— But, you can talk, eh?

— A pig grunting!...

— You can reason, eh?

— Now what is that?...

— We are human kind, I sure of that!...

— Look at the colour of my skin: that is the devil own colour!... You can see in the pictures!...

That man was suffering a terrible affliction: loss of self-respect. No one could make him believe that he was a man. It went with that other drastic loss: he couldn't remember anything. Not where he came from. Not the brown colour of the earth where he was born. Not the river running over the grey sand. Not the day he caught the truck coming into town. Nor the afternoon when the ambulance from the General Hospital carried him to the madhouse after they pulled him out of the latrine pit. He'd run away from the asylum because he couldn't stand living with crazy people. They were too ambitious and stuck-up. Some took themselves for magistrates, lawyers, doctors, taxi-drivers; other got themselves up as Heads of State. He found those ones altogether too foolish, they kept themselves to themselves like hurry-come-up lords, and gave orders with speechifying flapping of arms, all blown away on the breeze.

He was a lost man.

— Holy Virgin! What strange diseases men have. It is the end of the world!

She crossed herself.

Killer sickness. Plague. Blue fever. The grand parade where infectious evils thronged in their millions. It took the path to the shacks, rotted the planks, poisoned the fresh water in the fountain, wandered along the garbage-laden gullies, went and revived itself in the latrine pits, trickled along the gutters until it flew up in the air in a fabulous cloud of a billion nine hundred and ninety-five thousand flies and three billion six hundred and two thousand mosquitoes. This epidemic fauna gave concern to the experts, so those gentlemen compiled their statistics, with the help of an exhausting census of insect fertility in the metropolitan area.

The-man-who-couldn't-believe-he-was-a-man got out of the bus accompanied by a woman as silent as a tomb. They were disappointed by the vanity of human kind. They paid their fares like everyone else and went off with the wind inside them, like wandering souls.

People say they spent their lives going from one dirty place to another, reading the future from the shade of skins. The words from their lips struck fear into hearts. People tell how one day he told a fair-skinned man that he would be rich and wise: the man became a big merchant on the sea front and spent his time studying fish in an aquarium he set up somewhere. Another day, a dark-skinned man consulted him. The man gave a horrifed stare at the colour of his skin:

— Go and rub yourself with cornwood or you'll be unlucky! Unlucky!...

The dark-skinned man rubbed until his skin was raw. But

before a year was out, his body was found in his shack, eaten out and sucked dry by the bugs and the red ants, and stinking of piss and decay. His penis had gone completely, and where his eyes had been were just two holes where long trails of flesh-eating ants went out and in.

The-man-with-no-memory said that other one was mad, and the woman whose husband was beheaded in the cane plantations felt the cramp gripping her again.

— Driver, get your crate moving!

— How long this heap of scrap-iron been crawling along?

— And the man not even got him mind on him work!

Some yawned fit to break their jaws. Some gazed dolefully down at their sad dusty shoes. The women thought about the price of rice, and corn, soap and black peas, how they never stop going up. The eyes of the men were worn with their worries: the sickness, the house-rent, all the weariness that earned no pay, the dreadful look of children too weak to cry when foodtime echoes through their bellies, and the fear of malaria, because they have to sleep beside the pools of slimy stinking water where three billion six hundred and two thousand mosquitoes are hatching, and one million nine hundred and ninety-five thousand flies are growing fat.

Arms, hands, knees, legs and shoes.... The people who had lost their roots watched the ribbon of asphalt unrolling away beneath them, and those with memories dimly recalled a village in the fold of the hills, between the red blossoms of the flame-of-the-forest and the majestic ancient cotton-trees alive with singing birds. They remembered a cottage among the banana leaves, the brown of the earth and the river flowing over the black sand.

Displaced people don't want to remember. And when they do a foot shakes as if it's beating out the rhythm of the pain, they cup a hard jaw deep in the palm of a hand and pass around the cigarette to its last gasp.

Lost people—they don't like to weep.

And that's why, when their empty-belly children cry, they feel their head heavy like a charge of lead. They lose control and whip them to make them hold their noise. Their womenfolk don't dare say a word when the red rage takes hold. One of them hit his wife so hard that her tubes blocked off and never again could she have a child.

Lost people like to have plenty of children. Fornicate all the blessed day. Say it's their only hope: pickney like the fingers of your hand, faster than death can carry them off. And so the babies come, ten, twenty, thirty at a time. And as they grow they get to know the alleyways and hide-and-seek corners. Only they don't grow up like corn, they grow up like the shacks. Legs like the crooked posts that prop up the huts. Never have they had the smile of those boys bursting with health who are pasted up with starch to decorate the inside walls of the shacks.

And as the dispossessed arrive, so the shacks spring up like weeds. That's their only hope they say, breeding ten at a time, faster than death. The men are valiant enough to look into the sun. To flounder in the mud. The women are valiant enough to perfume with sweet-scented herbs and cheap lotions the rooms and beds where gloomy strangers will come and sprawl. When they can't take it any more, they play masquerade with turkey-feather hats and painted faces: or cup their jaw in the palm of their hand and stare at their bare feet, planted like the base of some sad statue on this plague-ridden swampy ground. Then they see again the painful death of a field burned by the sun. They can still smell it rotting. They remember the deserted cottages where donkeys covered with boils wander in and out of open doors.

Lost people don't want to remember. And, when they do, a fearful urge to smash tables pulsates through their veins and they pass around the cigarette to its last gasp.

— Thank you *m'sieu*. That make me feel better. I don't smoke since morning. You really can't remember where you come from?

— I really can't remember.

— I feel the gripe in me belly...

— Driver, get this crate moving!...

— I can feel a animal moving, here, in me chest!...

— You don't drink your coffee since morning. As for me...(he coughed) all I have since three days is cold water from the fountain. And I can feel...(he coughed again) me chest pulling in like elastic band!...

— Mebbe is gas. Me, I feel something shut up me chest like lock and chain.

— Driver, go on...(she gave a gulp) go on...the gripe's catching me too!

— Eeeh...Me too!

— M!...M!...Me too!

— Me too!

Every soul on the bus felt the gripes.

— Water! Me thirsty!...Water!...

This one had a thick white tongue hanging out over his lower lip. He clutched his chest as if he wanted to throw up the cold water from the fountain which was the only thing in his belly for three days.

Then the passengers looked from one to another as if a sudden madness was catching hold of them. They remembered the smell of the bodies drowned in the sewer and searched about if there wasn't a corpse among them beginning to rot. They pushed each other about. Stared nose to nose, eye to eye. And they squeezed the luggage with their thick hands to check what was inside. They hunted the corpse, snuffling at the baking air inside the bus. One slashed at a sack with his penknife. Out came corn. They pushed each other about. Silent. Tense. Fearful.

— The plague!...

The word vibrated in the air. Dry as a cough. Desperate as the day when the crowd came out to burn the bodies drowned in the drain.

Hair stood on end with fear.

The man with the knife looked at the others savagely like a mad dog. A woman threw herself out onto the asphalt and broke a bone. Then, caught up by some inner force, everyone struck fists against the glass and smashed it.

Astounded and sweating with rage, John stopped the bus. With one big jolt. The passengers got off, pushing each other about... Yelling curses at them, he tried to stop them as they ran away. A man who was sitting up front shouted that the splinters of glass had nearly wounded him. He hit out at the others. They showed him the woman lying in the road. She was groaning in her blood. John stopped, breathless. But the man in the front seat increased his violence, demented with rage.

He slapped the man-with-no-memory several times and pushed him around. He pulled a gun out of the belt of his trousers and struck a brutal blow on the forehead of the man-who-couldn't-believe-he-was-a-man. With a hard punch he split the lips of the woman-whose-husband-was-beheaded-in-the-sugarcane-plantations. With a kick in the belly, he made the man vomit who'd drunk only cold water from the fountain for the past three days.

Some of the passengers were smart enough to slip away with the help of the crowd who gathered at the bus to watch the show. The traffic cop on the corner wanted to take control of the whole business, but the gunman vigorously stopped him. Even so, when the gunman decided, as he said, to bring home the bacon, the cop got into the old Ford beside John. In the back there were the bits of baggage slit open, the woman in pain from her broken limbs being taken to the General Hospital, the-man-with-no-memory, the-one-who-didn't-belive-he-was-a-man, the woman-whose-husband-was-beheaded-in-Cuba, the man who for three days had only drunk cold water from the fountain, the one who slit the sacks with his knife and the gunman who had a fit because the glass splinters nearly cut him.

The bus went back the way it had come, creaking and

whining along the grey asphalt strip. John said to himself:

— But, is what the hell happen, Our Lady of Perpetual Help?...

She still beamed down, silent and serene, on the little cashbox, beside the golden spider's web. John felt a tear come to his eye. But lost people never weep. He swallowed back his mouth-water:

— Is what the hell happen? See how they done break the glass! What make the girl throw herself out on the road? Is what the hell happen?...

The bus returned the way it had come, creaking and whining...

The people inside had forgotten their gripes. The woman who had thrown herself out onto the road moaned like an animal. The one who first of all complained of cramp now only felt the bitter salty taste of blood on her lips:

— What time now, *m'sieu*?

— Don't you dare say a word!...shouted the gunman threateningly.

The man whose brow was bathed in blood looked indignantly at him and answered:

— Half past two, me dear.

The gun butt came down again on the wound.

Raphael was sitting on an upturned mortar.

The man gripped his waist between his legs like a pair of scissors. He made the boy's head froth up with lather, and using a piece of broken bottle he worked over the obstinate roots of hair with professional skill. Now and again Raphael pulled a face. The bit of bottle went back and forth from his forehead to the back of his neck, by way of his temples and his ear-corners. Once this operation was done, solemn as a monk, the man washed the head, which dried in the sun like a marble. Then he used a powder to give the bald pate a sweet smell.

— There you are, me son!

Raphael raised up his mirror-smooth head.

He twisted his face to try to catch the smell of the powder. But he was jumping for joy, and paid no mind to the racket of ten or so children who chased after him banging on cooking pots and chanting:

> *Shine-head baba,*
> *Penny cassada!*

He was only just ten and no taller than a little corn sprout. He'd seen nothing of the river or the red blossoms of the flame-of-the-forest. He'd grown among the shacks and shanties. And for want of the flame-tree and the river, he'd loved Father Leon's white pigeons. Far back in his farthest past there was a blank, except the day he was born, when the medical staff were all amazed: this newborn babe had such a stiff little sinting that not a soul could look upon it without collapsing in helpless laughter. Madeleine remembered the three days she had lain with his father, and when she was soothing the baby to sleep she would rock him to the tune of *Carolina Ac-ao* or *Pumpkin nebba bear calabash*....

He was named for good Raphael.

It took quite a time before he was given this name, because the baptism had to wait until the day when Erzulie would give the sign in a dream. Meantime, because he was already three, they called him, shouting it out as a bit of a joke, ''the little boy who loved pigeons''. But his father hit on a pet name after his own, and for the time being, while he waited to present him for christening, named him Johnny Dove; he was convinced that plague and disease could even infect his name. And he wanted to keep his son out of their reach. And so he traced indigo on the silk-red cloth in honour of the mistress of his dreams and his good fortune. One night of weariness and grief, for it had been a bad day and the old Ford had got a puncture, she came to him.

A tall woman with long braided jet-black hair, dressed in a blue robe scattered all over with stars, she resembled the Virgin of Guadelupe. She held up Raphael at her breast and when she opened her mouth to speak to John, clusters of yellow butterflies took flight from her lips and disappeared into the clouds. She demanded an abundance of wines, fresh fish, yams, iced cakes, chicken meat, pork, beef and white pigeons. She said to be sure not to forget the perfume.

And she faded away in a tinkling of gold bracelets and fallen stars.

John woke up to a scent of incense. He knew he had been too weighed down with weariness to burn any before falling asleep. He thought:

— That is Midsummer Day, the day of butterflies. We'll

christen Raphael on the twenty-fourth of June.

It was the twenty-fourth of May. John had only a month left to prepare for the festive day. First of all to find money for the big feast. Then to see about the official Catholic part. If Madeleine had still been there, she would have been a help to him, for besides being a good soul, she was a woman who busied herself about all the while. A pity. She had left and gone when the boy was one year old. John couldn't give her the five hundred gourdes she needed for something or other.

A dim memory came to him of her hips and the foot she used to rest on his hairy chest. Then he couldn't remember anything more and went back to sleep on his mattress smelling of piss, in the trembling light of the candle set in his prayer corner.

The bus didn't always run so good. All up and down he racked his brain to raise a loan. Playing the lottery more than ever according to his dreams. Two weeks gone by. He hadn't managed yet to make back the two hundred and fifty gourdes lost in two draws. He went to the cockfight to put money on the bold Spanish cock belonging to Brother Helophernes. And won eight hundred gourdes. That same day he very nearly stabbed one of the losers with a three-eighths stiletto he hid round his hips: in revenge for the money he was losing, the fellow reminded John, and made a lot of noise about it, that Johnny Dove mama was a good-time girl from the whorehouse.

On the twenty-second of June, while the cannon boomed out in celebration of a certain festival, and men in blue strolled along the lanes tickling the prostitutes, John went to market with one of his neighbours to buy fresh fish, bottles of white wine, a fat pig, all kinds of fruit, barley-water liqueurs and everything that might be pleasing to Erzulie-the-Great. When John and the woman got back, with a bearer in front, the neighbours met them with applause and helped them pull along the fat pig, which grunted at the barking dogs.

At last on the twenty-fourth when back from church, John, got up fine as a star in the sky in a suit that was a bit too big, the christening boy with his mirror-clean head and his Sunday best, the godfather and the godmother all appeared, they were amazed to find such a crowd waiting for them.

Lost people come from every alleyway could be seen, the little friends of the christened boy who shouted "Shine-head baba!" when he appeared, the barber who specialised in razor-path haircuts, Father Leon beaming away through his eighty-year-old wrinkles, so many happy people. With one accord they demanded to know the little boy's name. When they heard it was Raphael they clapped their hands fit to break and the urchins hammered out an infernal din on their pans. Only Father Leon felt disappointed. With that name he believed the boy would stop loving his gentle creatures. He left the crowd and went off to talk to his white pigeons. He didn't find them. Silent and full of woe, Father Leon decided that this christening could only bring him bad luck. He shut himself up in his little house to avoid hearing the sounds of the celebration.

The yellow midsummer butterflies flew over the old roofs.

The poor people held out their calabash bowls, and chicken legs, chunks of beef, and great spoonfuls of rice descended into them like manna from heaven. They tore the meat apart with ravenous teeth, wounding their lips and gums. Some who were tougher shoved away the weaker ones. Where you come from, they asked, you're not from here; and they thumped a few limbs in the confusion of the jostling. You could hear shrill cries. Groaning. It was all grease and sweat, fat pork and banggarang.

But where are they going, all the midsummer butterflies?

When the big feed came to an end, the crowd slowly drifted away to a sound of wood: crutches, sticks and bowls. Some of them went off with an extra pain or wound, but everyone with a full belly, and a few threw up the half of what they'd swallowed. The dogs barked at the procession as it passed down the narrow ways.

A shower of rain suddenly caught them, pelting down as if to wash away what can only happen one special day during the long years of old dreams and slow death. The overflowing sewer also had its big feed. Next day, dead bodies were found floating in the filthy water among the chairs, bits of plank and jumble of debris.

The next day had dawned dismally, and the doors were still wet when they were pushed open against the mud. The woman selling coffee was already settled in her corner. A sound of metal woke up the children: the hammer clang told of yet another shack going up somewhere.

Father Leon didn't open his door until he heard a rustle of wings by his window. Looking out, he saw the white pigeons. Raphael was already there.

— I thought you had forgotten them.

— They flew away because there was too much noise. But when I called them this morning, back they came.

And Father Leon crinkled up his eighty-year-old wrinkles in a smile again.

He was only just ten. Every day he had seen people come and plant their shacks everywhere about. He had seen dead bodies floating on the filthy water, seen men fighting with knives and pigeons flying off, never to return.

Raphael's little friends, weary at last of chasing after him down the alleyways beating their pans, scattered away in little groups, their bare feet thick with dust. A smell of fritters hung in the air.

Young girls half-naked coming back from the fountain with cans of water on their heads. Some with firm round breasts like shining apples and wet dresses clinging to the curve of their thighs. Others came talking about the Machine. It wasn't working so good. Gave you the backache. A cramp in the wrists. A heavy ache in your head. One said she couldn't take no more, she not going to finish all mash up by that machine handle. The same one spoke about Bernadette, how last year she caught the dry cough in her belly, and finish in the sanatorium throwing up blood. Another replied that the only thing to do was bear the cross, can't hope for nothing outside those six gourde fifty them pay. A hungry wage! Just enough to buy one potful of good corn! And they fell silent, scattering away down the alleyways between walls the colour of a sandal's sole.

John had got into the habit of coming home after four, with the last groups of factory girls. Raphael, dust between his toes and a grin on his lips, always expected him to come when they did. Although they felt so tired and gloomy when they took the path home by the shack, the factory girls used to call out to this little boy who met them every day.

That afternoon they could hardly recognize him, looking so fine with his mirror-clean head.

— Who peel you head, Raphael?

— You see Papa Djo coming? he asked.

They reached him, weary faces, crooked limbs, swearing like jailbirds.

— That Machine not working so good. Bernadette...

— You see Papa Djo coming?...

— Is that bookkeeper I can't stand. Every minute him eye on me. The fellow don't have no work to do?

— All right, make him work.... Maybe you sweet him!

— You see Papa Djo?...

— Finding a work, that is one problem. Working, that is another.

— All of them, same thing.

— Papa Djo, you see him?...

— And then, see how they get rid of the woman that talk up all the while about the wages. I wonder what she going do with herself, poor thing.

— They are pigs.

— You see the bus name *Our Lady*?

— True word. You know what happen? She went off somewhere to make a complaint. Seems she didn't get through. She dragging herself about the street like a lost soul. She shamed to beg, it not nice to see at all!...

— But what we can do against the Machine. Is not as if I love it. I would dash it down any time, but....

— Please, you don't see....

The last girl had gone by. The afternoon was dying away behind the roofsheets in blazing crimson clouds. Raphael suddenly felt very alone. He looked all around, anxious.

He ran off at full speed and stopped breathlessly in front of his father's shack. It was still shut up.

It had a green door which opened on a narrow track, a window over the gully, a hole in the roof for the rain, the stars, the night-dew and the rats; above the green door a cross was marked in charcoal for Jesus' name, and a blue silk kerchief devoutly pinned up by the corners for Erzulie-

25

the-Great. In spite of seven years of rain, mud and sun, the little house stood more or less upright, though the sides had lost their colour, bleached paler than moonshine in July.

Disappointed, Raphael looked down at an old cooking pot in the doorway and with a kick sent it rolling along in the dust.

The sun slipped down behind the rusty roofs, night was spreading like the shadow of an old hat. All around came the sound of voices, laughter, wild curses. Crude insults. The clack of a domino on a bare table. Children bawling. Dogs barking.

The gas lamps were lit, and the drum sounded to signal nightfall. An old transistor groaned out the song of the dispossessed, it lingered on the air like citronnella. The first time we hear that tune, it seem as if the lost people's spirit awake. Who squatting down stand up, a hammer in their hand. The blind want to see and water come in their eye they rub so hard. Mouth open wide, they reach out far with their hand, like they trying to catch hold of this thing that passing away. The children hush their play, people everywhere coming to look out of their doorway and their window. Deep inside they feel the motion. Then out, out it bursts from their lips.

Rain a wet me, me have no roof
Sun a burn me, me have no roof
De work so hard, woi! de pay so small
Wha fe do to reach back home...

And sang they sang. And didn't stop till the rain beat down on the roofs. Lost people only fear the overflow drain. The echo of their voices died away as the fear of death caught their throats.

They passed the half-smoked cigarette from one to the next. Their song tasted of white rum, bitter brew and punch.

The cigarette butt glowed from lip to lip, down to the last gasp.

Raphael sat himself down in front of the door on an old herring box. Eyes fixed on his toes in the dust, elbows on knees, jaw in the palm of his hand. already he sat as the others sit when their head is heavy.

Time passed.

The stars came out like camelias. Raphael leant his back against the door. And his head began to nod.

Between the last buzzing of the flies and the first glittering of the stars could be heard the voice of the slum storyteller:

"...There is a little path that leads in the night to the voodoo *hounfort* where every Tuesday there is dancing in honour of Ogun. And every Tuesday down this path come the virgins in white dresses come to dance around the fire and stamp their heels on the beaten earth of the temple floor. Like the mortar pounding. They are born to be possessed by the fire and feel the cool earth under their feet. They are born to be possessed. By the flame. And by the dust. The living don't want the dead to know the coffin or hear the speeches: they are the people of earth and fire. Everywhere the earth is the same dust colour. Everywhere the fire shines with the same light. These people burn their dead and stir their ashes in the dust. In their shrines they light candles which never disappear but burn down little by little every time death strikes a member of the great family of earth and fire people, more numerous than the great phantom horde of the mosquitoes and the flies. That is why the great family burn their dead and love to have plenty of children. So that the candle never die. Eternity of fire. The body is joy and revival. What the factory machine breaks down is reborn every Tuesday at midnight, among the smells of burning oil and incense, in the trance, the bathing of the head, the chants, until being is transformed and the stars fall. Life is a blossom-tree. Life is a river....

"...There is a little lane winds between the huts and goes down to the river. The river flows between green fields that hide the colour of the earth. It flows among the hills as if slipping between the legs of a woman. With the same slowness. With the same dreams of clouds and birds. With the same power. And the corn grows. And the heart catches flame. And life catches flame: there are bare black children bathing in the river's icy flow. There are women with terracotta skins washing linen on white stones with soap and laundry blue, singing gentle songs and beating the wet linen with wooden paddles. There is this sad little girl singing *Eel in de water* as she fills her gourd with the fresh spring water, and she catches a glimpse of a strange naked woman, sitting over there on a rock and combing out her hair. The river flows like a light. Flows like a brightness. The sad little girl has grown. The day she saw blood in her panty, she was afraid and went to rub away the blood in the cold river water. And there on the rock where the woman was letting down her hair she saw, she saw the yellow comb with its slender shining teeth. She grabbed it up and wrapped it tight in her wet panty. The comb was cold like a fork in the rain. She hid it in the straw of her sleeping mat. And every night she sees, she sees a woman holding a piece of white linen spotted with blood, a beautiful woman pleading, pleading. She's never said a word about it to her parents. One day they took the rocky road and crossed where the big pool used to be; the river had dried up and the plants were dying. They passed right beside the rock with the donkey that carried their parcels. And the little girl saw the woman with the stained piece of linen, watching sadly as they passed. They went away towards the shacks, the parents with their donkey, the girl with the comb. One afternoon on the way back from the fountain, she saw the woman sitting in an alleyway with her blood flowing out. She soaked up the blood with the scrap of sodden linen. She wiped her legs and the blood still flowed. It was only that day that the parents of the little girl discovered that her period had started and that she had lost blood going to fetch water at the fountain. She grew tall, she grew tall like a little orange tree. She grew more beautiful. And out of fear, her parents hid her away...''

The old storyteller, carried away by his tale, took a deep breath before calling out to his listeners:
— *Crick*!
— *Crack*! came the response.
— *Virgin Mary petticoat full a fire-fly*!....
— *Stars in de sky*, came the answer all around.

The minute he laid his hand on his son's shaved head, John only dimly remembered the terrible burdens and troubles of the day. He gave a faint smile.
— Papa, said Raphael.
— Yes.
— You see I get me head shave, just like you want.
— That's good.
He stroked the shaven head.
— Papa!
— Yeah?
— Why you come home so late?

— I had a breakdown.

— Rubber burst again?

Smoke came drifting down the alley.

— That old crate don't want to shift herself again!

— Is when you going teach me to drive? I want to help you.

— You not old enough for that. Must keep going to school. I don't want you to finish up bus-man.

— Why, Papa?

— Bus make too much noise. Complaining like a sick woman. You would be afraid. That machine falling to pieces.

— I no fraid a nothing.

— I know that.

— So why you drive the machine?

John didn't know what to answer.

The old storyteller went on between the plumes of his cigarette smoke:

"...And no more water came from the fountain for many a long year. The men of earth and fire who feared the rain said prayers. In their devotions they prayed for heavy rain, even if many drowned bodies had to be burned at the sewer mouth. Water was for sale. And the price was high. Dust from the alleyways coated every lip. The shacks twisted up like a cactus field. Every man among the rootless ones felt his tongue stir in the back of his mouth like that of an ox. Thick. Heavy...coated over. White as starch. Making him spit on his wine-coloured piss frothing in the dust. It was in that season of burning thirst that they began to kill the dogs. The ones that foamed at the mouth, drawing behind them the army of one million nine hundred and ninety-five thousand flies. Strange to say, the day when twenty dogs were beaten to death with sticks and stones was the day of the Massacre of the

Holy Innocents. They were buried in a common grave. And a clump of wild flowers that sprang up where the dirt was turned long marked the spot where the dogs had fallen. There was a mad woman all rag and bone who used to come to weep on the wild flower plot, with her bundle clanking of cauldrons. Old Hag they called her. And the children were afraid of her toothless gums. And the men scattered salt when she passed. People kept the memory of the day of the massacre of the dogs. Every year a jug of water was emptied over the wild flower plot. Years passed. No one kept up the ritual of the water for the dogs. And every day people came and put up shacks. Soon the only place left was the wild flower plot. A man from Bombardopolis came with his wife and put up a shack on the place of the wild flowers. They saw people staring at them, but never understood why. After ten months, the wife gave birth to a little puppy dog. Together they strangled it and buried it under their beaten earth floor. But every night they heard a scratching of claws at the bottom of their door and the whining of a little dog. One night the man armed himself with a big stick and opened the door. He saw a big white dog sitting on its tail watching him. In silence. And a shadow with a human shape clattering pans. The man worked some *obeah* to keep the evil spirits away from their shack. And for a good while he didn't hear the scratching of the claws and the whining of the dog. After twelve months, the woman again gave birth to a puppy. They buried it in the same spot. And that same night they left the shack and went away. They left between two big white dogs and they heard amid the clatter of pans the grating cackle of an old hag. Next morning the wild flowers began to spring again on the patch of dirt among the rotting planks, the termites and hundreds of earthworms.

"The fountain gave no water and the people stayed indoors. They were frightened of the noonday sun. They stayed inside their hovels keeping company with sweat, worry and fretting, thirst and disease. If they ventured out, it was to study the colour of the clouds and feel the dust, fine like woman's facepowder, trickling through their hands.

"At the end of three years, two months, three weeks and four days, one breezy dusty day, down the path that leads to the fountain came a beautiful brown girl with long braids of black hair hanging down her back. That afternoon the sky grew dark and the long-awaited rain fell for a week. And the rain smashed down the makeshift huts, washed away man and beast and left a thick layer of mud on the wild flower plot where on the day of the Massacre of the Holy Innocents the dogs had been buried. The corpses were counted and thrown into a ten-foot grave."

— *Crick*!
— *Crack*!
— *Two foot can't fit in one shoe....*
— *Must can fit in de coffin*!"

The old storyteller hushed his mouth.
The stars spread over the azure sky like camelias. And the darkness glowed, transparent as angel palaces, reaching back eternally in the night of time.

He needed a paper to cross to the other side of the country. And he was one of the first to hear his name and number spelt out among the fifteen thousand men come to look for work. They came from everywhere, anyone who had hands and arms, a huge movement of poor people. The slums emptied out one day only to fill up again next morning when the trucks came in and unloaded their cargo of bones and arms and grimy drinking gourds and bundles all muddy and dusty but haloed around with high hopes.

King Cane wanted hands for the harvest.

Their hands were big and broad, could hold a machete and swing it in the air like a greeting to the sun. Old General-Sun! Thick heavy paws with hard patches and nails, hanging down empty like uprooted tree-trunks. Anytime they closed for a while around a bottle of white rum, next thing it would get smashed. Anytime they grappled rootlike fingers on a woman's breast or belly, next thing she would get hurt.

King Cane wanted hands.

The old storyteller told anyone who would hear about the hell of the sugar plantations. Dead men dumped in carts to be burned with the cane trash. Hands crushed. Bodies burnt. Penises cut off. Balls roasted. Thousands of lives gone up in flames. And all that blood dug into the ground to fertilise new plantations stretching acre after acre in the heat, sweat and flies. They said he had a mouth like running belly, that he was a chattery fool, that old tale-teller. The official story made it known no blood had been shed.

King Cane needed that version of the story.

For they still need those big paws that know how to swing a machete. And those big paws kept on coming, perched on trucks, hanging on to the dusty creaking bodywork that left long trails of rags on potholed roads. They were sick of pulling a barrow over the tarmac of city streets. Struggling up the slopes, straining their chests, they retrod the road to Calvary. Two wheels trundling along with bumps and crude repairs, held up by crooked axles. Two wheels trundling along every street. Dust, mud and tar, wrists, legs and sacking: the handcart creaked along, with the dogs behind it and a strong smell of sweat. For sure they couldn't take no more. The handcart was left in its owner's hands, and they went off to get the paper with your name and number that let you get across to the other side of the country. Under the bridges they slept. In church porches. In dark corners of the old port. In markets. On the sidewalks.

King Cane wanted hands.

A man went to market with a few bottles to sell to buy healing oil for his sick woman. He'd heard about the work and he went across the border without even carrying home the oil to his wife. Men came from the wide plains, emerging from the slopes of the sun like ragged scraps of sorrow. The main road spewed them out, like an overstuffed belly. A procession of sores and decay. They got acquainted with brawny fists. Cébien Lagrenade. Servilus Dieusifort. Odilon Mérilis. Aristide Lapongnette. Vilbrin Granchimin. Juscaubout Naviré. Joseph Beaufort. Joachim Gentilhomme. Lifet Bienvenu. Montilas Eliézer. Vénel Paul. Viénèg Mesidor. Dieudunor Dorélien. And all the others who didn't know each other but travelled the same unhappy road.

King Cane wanted arms.

And for days on end the main road spewed them out. In the sun. In the dust. Wheels creaking. And the months went by with a smell of sweat, blood, bruises and fires. And with waiting for the end of the contract time came nostalgia. The storyteller told anyone listening about the hell of the cane plantations. It was then that the men returned to see the dried up river, the parched grass, the bare fields, the dusty blackened hovels. The man who'd gone for healing oil brought a sewing-machine for his wife. He couldn't find her anywhere. It was grief had carried her off, more than the chest disease. The man didn't even have the luck to see the little house he'd left behind. It had gone up in flames with hundreds of others, one afternoon in June.

A fellow with a scar on his right cheek got off a truck on the outskirts of the capital. Just by the roadside he shook out his pipe and buttoned up his fly.

He was one of the first of the fifteen thousand men to come back from the other side. *Virgén Altagracia,* Holy Mother of God! All the time he'd wanted to fight it out with the boss's strong-arm men, but they'd given him a final chop with the knife, leaving that deep, deep scar in his right cheek. It would brand him for the rest of his days. In spite of all the care he'd had from the 'paniard girl with skin like ripe corn who called him *hombre mío* and wept as she sponged that horribly split face of his. She'd begged him not to make trouble when she saw how much bad blood he had for that rass of a *capataz* overseer. But she still hid him away when the *Guardia* were hunting him: he'd killed that *capataz* on the spot with a machete chop in the chest. The Dominicano had cynically burned his back with a lighted cigar, cursing him all the while for a filthy *negro* bastard. Together they had fled across the fields and plains, sleeping one night with one peasant, and tomorrow with another, and after that in a wood: wading through the swamps, stung by mosquitoes, lashed by rains, torn by the *macca*-bush or roasted by the sun. The Pedernales River was their hope, flowing over the white pebbles like a ribbon of pure light. He was one of the five organisers when the farm workers went on strike and paralysed a whole area of the feudal domain.

One very hot night, Antonio had been stabbed three times. Dorilon's body had been found in a whore's bed, blood trickling from the mouth. They'd fished Cassagnol's corpse out of the mosquito pond, covered in stinking mud. Dieuveut's head had fallen in a cane field, to be eaten away by the mad ants. As for him, the *capataz* had been ordered to work him over, before they finished him off whatever way appealed to their imagination. He'd repaid his insolence with that machete blow.

Hombre mío, I'm so tired. The woman the colour of ripe corn lay down in the open and the man kept watch, his machete still smeared with the overseer's blood.

They started out again with the sun beating down. Their memory still throbbed with the birdsong in the woods and the strong scent of wild flowers, moist earth and sap. Worn out, with thick-coated tongues, they had seen the Pedernales a few steps away, one fresh morning full of frogs croaking. The river was beautiful. White as milk. With red flame-tree blossoms floating on calm waters. Just a few steps away flowed the Pedernales, so beautiful. They had caught sight of freedom. Her man had often talked to her about it, but she'd never understood what it could be. She gave herself to anyone who wanted. The man called it the water to quench the thirst of the fields, lovelier than the *Virgén Altagracia*. The man said that....that it was for her sake he was organising the struggle against the *capataces*. That day she understood. Even though they had walked two days and two nights, losing track of sun and moon, with the river always there, just a few steps ahead of them. Thick and yellow was the milk they'd drunk at the home of Manuelo, the old farmer who'd cured their roasting fever with bush-tea and oil-of-fitness. They'd gone on again when their strength returned.

Three weeks and two days they had been on the run when they saw the Pedernales again, not as beautiful as the river of their memories, among the birdsong and machine gun fire. Then the woman the colour of ripe corn remembered walking two days and two nights without stopping and she didn't want to go on. She thought it must be another mirage. And yet, still they kept on towards the Pedernales.

They drew near. A sound reached them along the river. A sound of boots. She was afraid. *Hombre mío.* The boots came closer. He flung himself into the river as a hail of machine gun bullets pierced the breast of the corn-ripe woman. The man dived into the Pedernales with a shoe from his woman mowed down at the water's edge. It was only the power of his arms and the endurance of his lungs that saved his life as the crocodiles and alligators hunted him down.

When at last he could feel underfoot the land of his own country, he collapsed like an old sack, using his last strength to clutch the shoe of the woman who had helped him escape the *Guardia.* Just before he was overcome by a heavy fainting sleep Dorilon, Antonio, Cassagnol and Dieuveut passed through his mind, all fine comrades who held their heads high; Manuelo who'd cared for him in his simple hut, and his 'paniard girl the colour of ripe corn named María Isabel. The *Guardia* put about the rumour he was dead, burned with the cane trash. All the Haitian *braceros* knew the *Guardia* still searched for him, not believing he could still be alive, and what's more, across the border.... Rolling home down the main road, against the orders of all the sergeants at checkpoints their truck passed through, the *braceros* sang a tune they used to sing softly over there at night in the fields:

> *Can't tek dis life no more, oh!*
> *Can't tek dis life no more, mi friend*

You turn dis way, water is here
Turn dat way, more water dere
Gwine tek rockstone full up de sea oh
Can't tek dis life no more oh!

The man came back at the time of the great drought. He couldn't recognize the shacks veiled over with dust. The dogs went by frothing at the mouth or pissing in corners. Men who were nothing but skin, bone, whiskers, teeth and nails dragged their carcasses over ground the colour of volcanic tuff. Sometimes one would fall down suddenly in the dust, heat-struck. Dogs would sniff and then pass on, whining, muzzles pointing to the sun. The men feared this howling of dogs which went on until the first gleams of moonrise. And they came out from their hovels, like beasts from their holes, a patchwork of rags and curses, flinging rocks to demand silence in the hot night.

Night full of stars.

He had lived through the hell of the feudal domain and walked for three weeks and two days under the fiery rays of the sun and the blue light of the stars, pursued by tracker dogs, bullets and boots. So the man of Pedernales often called to mind Dorilon, Dieuveut, Cassagnol, Antonio, the whore María Isabel, riddled with bullets on the other side of the river, her memory staying with him as a smell of woman and baked earth. How she used to rest the soles of her warm feet on his hairy chest. Now *Wet-Back* (so they named him after the story of his swim across the border) had returned to his dispossessed brothers whose dust and smell sprawled across the city like the passing of a terrible comet.

After three years, two months, three weeks and four days of dryness it rained without ceasing for seven days and seven nights.

On the first day dark clouds appeared, never seen in the sky during the long season of drought. Then fine drops began to fall, drawing forth the smell of the earth to a great shout of deliverance. People came out into the lanes and the alleys stretching out their mouths to the clouds to drink the drops of warm water falling on the ghetto. There was an overcast sun like a brownskin girl. And the air was a yellowish pink like brickdust. The strong smell of the earth rose up towards flaring nostrils. And no one was afraid to pluck the wild flowers from the dogs' burial plot, and cast them towards the clouds. With the same gesture they pointed at the rainbow, arching its bridge of many-coloured splendour over the wet shacks, like the sash of the Virgin of the Rosary. Some people talked about the brown girl they had seen. Others believed it was a zombie beating his wife behind the shacks. Is lang time, eh-hey! he don't give the woman plenty licks for the hot little pum-pum she have. Sure thing she start to carry-on again. But when they saw the rain fall without ceasing, they crossed themselves. With the right hand for thirst and the living. With the left hand for the dead and the fever coming.

On the second day, the hail rang down on the roof sheets with an interminable jangling. In the distance a church bell was ringing, as if in answer to the heaven-sent release. Naked children ran about in the rain with pans to catch the ice marbles falling from the clouds. But for the men the first heedless joy was already over and they listened to the force of the rain on the roofs and the wind roaring like the throb of an old engine. They listened as if it came from within their own chests. The church bell was still chiming. The jangling hail still cascaded down. And the men listened.

Hush your mouth women when the men are listening out.

On the third day once again not a soul ventured out. Big stones were rolled into place behind the doors, and those who had windows opened them to let the wind blow through. Blankets of black cloud hid the sun. For the last two days, the people shouting had quieted down, for the sound of the water began to rumble at the mouth of the drain. Out into the drenching rain and the grumbling thunder, men came naked and gleaming like worms, determined to use pickaxes, shovels and pikes to struggle against the blocking of the drain. The monster growled, if to scare away these men who were interfering with its raging, seething maw. In the putrid mud they unearthed with their picks jawbones of dogs and human skulls, deeply disturbing to look upon. Exhausted by the monster's violence, they went back to their huts, set down the washed and whitened skulls on a bare table and listened to the growling of the beast at the mouth of the drain.

On the fourth day, they went out again with pickaxes, shovels, pikes. And the beast swallowed them up. A great howl rose up among the people, drowning for a while the raging of the storm and the rumbling of the drain. Pathetic groups waded through the lanes thigh-deep in water, hands behind their heads. They drew close to the terrible maw.

All they could see were the pick handles still sticking out of the ground before being completely engulfed, with a dog's skull perched on one of them, like a spear for some magic ritual piercing straight to the heart of their misery. They drew back when the monster growled.

On the fifth day lightning split the sky with fantastic flashes. The children cried out. The women prayed to the Holy Virgin. The men listened. Over there a board cracking. Right here a zinc sheet grating. Farther off the the grumbling of the beast that had swallowed their comrades. And the wind passing through the windows with a fierce whistling.

The water began to invade the homes.

Men, women, boys and girls fought to bale it out again with bowls, dishes and beakers.

The water didn't want to leave. It rose higher.

The Dieudonné family lost their three-month-old child. Choked by the beast. The woman clutched the dead baby to her bony breast. Dieudonné wept as he emptied the filthy water out of the window.

On the sixth day, a thunder-stone fell. As it fell it knocked down four huts. And where it passed ploughed up a wide trench which in no time filled up with water. Then shacks set sail on the water like boats. They caught against tree trunks or were sucked down under the water. When evening came, there was a calmer spell in the heavens. And on the earth.

On the seventh day, the waters rested.

The church bell pealed out again in the joy of deliverance, but it rang like a hollow laugh over a doom-stricken landscape.

In the evil slime that had flowed into the hovels and covered the passageways, people looked for dead babies. Chairs. Simple homely things. Some men were ready to dive into the water-filled dike to fish out the thunder-stone. The Good Lord stamp him foot too hard, fe true. Him don't love poor people. So thought John as he stepped over the puddles of stinking mud with Raphael on his shoulders to go and look at the body of the toothless old hag among the twenty or so victims drowned at the mouth of the drain.

No one had seen the bodies of the comrades lost on the fourth day. While they were using a branch to search for them, the old hag floated to the top of the filthy water with a ghastly skeleton's grin. She was horribly naked. And what most caught the eye was the pubic bone of her bald cunt. The crowd stoned the body and the rocks rattled on her bones as on a tin beaker. The people pulled her out of the dirty water and laid her out in the sun, like an offering to the Lord of the Rain. For ever since the day when some believers heard the parish priest preaching about witches who bring misfortune to men, the whole slum had heard the word. And the only reason the people hadn't stoned her while she was alive was from fear of giving birth to puppy-dogs or having *obeah* put on them by her evil powers. They fixed the body to an old door. That way two men bore the body on their shaved heads, dancing along and refreshing themselves with white rum. The noisy procession climbed up the highest place in the shantytown. There the door was nailed to a pole for all to behold the body crucified. And so that the stench of rotting could be smelled in heaven. And in memory of that day, the hilltop was named Death's-Door.

To climb up towards Death's-Door, you have to take the passageway called Seven-Dagger-Cut, which leads into Sorrow-Alley, passes behind the fountain and comes out at the long mud pond like a plague-ridden backwater. It was in this silt-coloured place that the latest comers, unable to find another square of ground, built their shacks—and proved their resourcefulness by driving their cornerposts into this vile swamp which smelled so violently of human and animal shit. Often a dense column of smoke rose up from this part, and no one could ever understand how the people there made fire in their world of wood and water. It was there too that you most often heard children shouting and the bawling of newborn babes. There could be found a colony of tall strong black people with blue-black skins. They spoke an unusual Creole, and all had bald heads gleaming like polished stone. It was two of them who danced with the door and the Old Hag's body. People pointed them out when they passed. Because of the smoke they made every day on their stinking swamp, people called them the Mosquito-Hunters.

It was due to their initiative that you no longer saw all along the mud pond, the puckering of painful arseholes, creased-up bellies and straining ribs at each press to defecate. They dug a deep trench in the mud and using what came to hand, put up some little shelters where you could come and ease yourself for ten cents the half-hour. They put down boards to keep your feet dry. And planted rose laurels and yellow leaf shrubs where the mud had dried.

When John came this way he remembered the long mud pond where the pigs came to wallow among the flies, mosquitoes and rats. As he went through the quarter there were whitewashed cottages with flocks of pigeons flying over them in the pale dawn light. From the day before the house fronts had been swept, the ground watered, the tables dusted.

It was a Sunday, and John was visiting Passiona.

She sold chains, necklaces, finger rings, earrings, bracelets, pinchbeck trinkets, madras headties in every colour, little vials of scent: her booth was like a fairyland of lights. She traded on the sea front. The place smelling of seaweed, spices and onion where the foreigners in exotic costumes—sandals on their feet and turbans on their heads—would eventually settle down, they who came from unknown lands with their bears, monkeys, parrots, and ever a box on their backs. Passiona also sold booklets of prayers and litanies for

43

church novenas, scapulars, paper pictures, good-luck charms. She read the future if you asked her. She lived in the quarter in one of the little white houses built on the site of the pig wallow.

The door was still shut and Passiona was dreaming about her marriage on the waters of the Artibonite river: on a clear afternoon, all fresh and sweet-scented, she was sailing along on the silent waters with her man beside her, the breeze swelling her white bridal veils and the rosy sunlight powdering her face.

When he pushed open the creaking door, John found her on her old mattress with a tear trickling gently down her cheek.

Three years had gone by already since the gunman had injured John's passengers. Passiona's tear suddenly brought to his mind the terrible heat of that June day and the thick clot of blood on the mouth of the woman whose husband was beheaded in a cane plantation. The story Passiona often told to John was a little like that woman's: her man had gone for a spin in a sailing ship that never reached the Bahamas. Shipwrecked on the high seas. The pretty trinket-seller often thought about it. John had not so far taken the place of the shipwrecked man who haunted her memory.

Outside the shantytown was waking up, weary to the bones, like an old whore. Sundays let out poverty like a running belly. The sound of a church bell could be heard in the distance. Cocks crowed in a gloomy world. A little boy played a flute as he wandered down the passageways.

On the bed, Passiona was still dreaming. John shook her by the shoulder:

— Cock a crow. You weeping, Passiona.

It seemed the red sun was setting behind the river.

— Dulménise mek her strong coffee already. Sun up, Passiona.

The sky lost its rosy hue. The flowers in the boat suddenly shrivelled. And Passiona's bridal dress dropped away like a dove fallen from an old tree. All that lingered was the scent of mint: she'd brought a root in her bundle and it grew in a corner of the room.

They had met as if by chance. And John breathed in that scent he had missed for long years. She'd showed the man the way that led to her little white house. Passiona had left her door open since nightfall but he only came in the pale early dawn.

— Why you come so late! said the woman rubbing her eyes.

— Sun up, Passiona.

— For me, night time was sooner.

— And why you crying in you sleep?

— Mebbe I dream a sad thing. I don't remember the dream. Long time now I don't remember what in dreams. Why you come so late? If you did come for the night I wouldn't cry. I wait for you and I watch through the window the star them bright behind Death-Door. Then I shut my old window. And I remember....

John lifted the iron hinge and pushed out the window. Thousands of tiny shacks, in the pale dawn light, were scrambling up the crest of Death's-Door. The bell sound died away in the distance. The melody of the flute flowed into the little room.

— I prefer you don't remember, Passiona!

— Yes, is so you always say. And, Holy Virgin, I know it hurt you...but I can't forget when I spend the night all alone....

— Raphael has the fever and he coughing a little. I was to stay with him. Dormelia, the laundress at the prison, she is watching him while I'm away. You know I can't tell you a lie, Passiona. When she hear about Raphael fever, Dormelia she burn the policeman khaki under the iron. She is a good woman, that Dormelia.

— And you didn't think to knock on my door?

— I was thinking....

John, all embarrassed, looked at the window hinge still swinging.

— What you say, John?

— I was thinking, mebbe, there was another man....

— John, no! You don't know me. I don't let them come to my house again. I want to live now like a honest woman with me earring and me kerchief. You can see, this life no give me nothing.

— Since when you decide this?

— I forget. It just come to me. I have enough. You see this piece of board? That is blood from bedbug all over there. But I never can save up a few gourdes to get the place whitewash: have to buy soap and perfume and bra and panty by the dozen to sweet the man and make them come back. All man want is we flesh. Don't give one rass for the bug crush on the board. Just want to poke it into we, that's all! And I remember....

— Passiona!

— Is how the hell me going stop remember? One time life wasn't like this. The rice did smell good and didn't cost much. You could have respect and mek your life according to how your family raise you!...Oh! beg pardon, John. I shouldn't get vex with you.

She threw herself into his arms. And John smelled the scent of mint in her hair.

— Now Passiona, you not going bawl again.

— John.

— Yes?

— You can bring you son here if you want. I will care him.

John had wanted to hold her close. And his heart beat like a young colt. Passiona pushed him gently away. The window hinge had stopped swinging.

— Fetch your boy now.

John pushed open the creaking door. And dashed through the narrow ways to his shack.

Raphael was lying on an old mattress, wrapped in a piece of coarse linen. Dormelia had brought her board and was using it to press a faded uniform, while she kept glancing at the child who coughed from time to time. John bundled him up in the white cloth that the laundress had spread over her ironing board.

— That air cool! Must keep him warm, Djo.

When John opened the door again, with his son in his arms, he stumbled into a rabble of naked children calling to Raphael with the din of their pans.

— Raphael sick, shouted John.

The kids fell quiet when they saw the white sheet. Only a dog still barked.

Is the measle your boy have. You must give him a bath of the blue wisteria, but there's no sun today.

John hurried off to search the thickets for the plant Passiona spoke of. Some poor people coming from the southernmost tip of the country had brought it in their bundles and planted it at the corner of their homes. It had grown up the old mud-brick walls and blossomed over the whitewashed huts. But a few months later, scorched by the sun and dust, the plant had dried up and died there on the old walls. John found the blue wisteria on the upper slopes of Death's-Door, among the caper flowers, redcoat-berries, crown-of-thorns, wild hog-plum, back-a-yard quinine and the yellow threads of love-bush twining between the twigs of shoe-black hibiscus with its red flowers. While he was tearing off the leaves and pricking his fingers on the thorn-bush, the sun came out and shone brightly over the hut roofs.

Passiona had already put out the water to sun in a white basin. When John arrived with the bush he found Raphael deathly pale, like bleached-out linen, and still coughing.

—It not good, Passiona. Him losing him colour and the cough keep racking him body.

She was already crushing the leaves vigorously in the water. It was in the little yard behind the white cottage.

Pieces of white linen smelling of soap were hanging from a scrap of line and silently weeping drops of blue-tinted water. Behind the house the water was warming in the sun in a white enamel basin. Passiona with her head tied up in a blue kerchief, hummed a washerwoman's song and waited to hear the noonday bell. It chimed out over the shanties then faded away like a dying bird. John brought out Raphael. Passiona plunged him into the warm water and rubbed over every part of his body with the blue wisteria and the other bush John had brought.

As night was falling, when John left Passiona's little house, she stopped him at her creaking door and said:

—You will come tomorrow, early early.

—Daybreak I will see you, Passiona, before I go look for Monday life.

—Listen now, John.

—Yes.

—Your boy there, you must protect him from harm.

—What are you saying, Passiona?

—Simbie-Mistress-of-the-Water already protect him. The drain can't touch him. But he need protection.

—Him safe with you Passiona....

Swaddled in the white cloth, Raphael had slept right through the night and hadn't heard the sound of tired wings beating at the closed window. Passiona woke at daybreak to prepare him hot tea. Dawn was breaking behind Death's-Door. When she passed near the window she saw a pigeon's body under the rose laurel. With an old kitchen knife she dug into the earth and buried the dead bird under the bush, face up to the sky. Then she crossed herself, looking toward the stars as they faded away in the blue light of dawn.

The powerful HASCO* siren vibrated through the morning.

The tractors had pushed them off this piece of land and out towards the sunswept salt flats and old mosquito swamps; then men had churned up the bowels of the earth to build great grey identical sheds with the sign on them saying INCORPORATED. Those who had been pitched out and could barely read the large letters of the sign were left darkly confused. Some said they were hospital buildings. Others that they were slaughterhouses, and wrote IN-CORPORATED with sticks in the dust to prove their point. They all agreed: *corpse* was a word heavy with meaning.

One morning where the road disappeared into the distance a thick cloud of dust stirred, moving closer with a confused uproar of whips cracking and animal sounds. A huge crowd appeared, followed by goats, pigs and cows, drawing a heavy procession of dust, bleating, grunting, moo-ing and loud argument right up to the gate of the big sheds. The men in charge, already informed but very surprised, came out to ask for an explanation from the other side of their padlocked gate.

— We come to sell we animal for meat!

*HASCO-Haitian American Sugar Company. INCORPORATED also suggests the Port-au-Prince Free Enterprise Zone.

The goats bleated. The pigs grunted. The cows mooed. And the men yelled out:

— Look here now. She breeding. A beast with plenty fat!

— Seventy-five gourdes for her.

— Look at this animal.

— Five dollars for a haunch of beef!

— Give me your price. Between us we can do a deal!

The goats bleated. The pigs grunted. The cows mooed. The ropes kicked up the dust. The men haggled.

The deafening racket went on for half an hour until a truckload of police arrived and charged the crowd, beating them with batons and rifle butts.... They battered away angrily among the stinking cow-pats and pig manure that dirtied them. The crowd scattered in complete confusion.

Later it took imagination on the part of the factory owners to get across to those who had been evicted without shelter that here you could get hired and put your hands on a paypacket. They ran a publicity campaign to convince people who were only just getting over their battering with police batons. And realising the source of the misunderstanding, they even pronounced it *Incorrperaytid* so that the dispossessed would understand it wasn't a slaughterhouse for animals.

Eventually they were convinced. And hundreds of them came to call out in the yard of the big sheds for this hiring of workers. They had turned their animals loose in the Grasspiece, for it was the factory that was going to provide for painting up your shack and buying yourself an old bed.

Dinombien, whose wife had wept the whole night long when he'd carried off their skinny old cow towards the sheds, he was still convinced they slaughtered beasts. He was about to prove it that morning while the woman accused him of having already forgotten how the police had driven off man and beast from the gate. Yet when the six o'clock siren went, with the taste of white rum in his mouth, he was setting off for there again. That was the only thing he could find to do, old Dinombien. And the men in the big sheds knew it. As for Dinombien, he had got used to seeing his shoes dragging along through the thick layer of fine dust. One day on that dusty road, the worker Dorismé approached him.

The old sun on the way to work. The years that only added more holes to tighten his belt. Holes in his pockets. His gaping poverty. Thrown up. Swallowed back. His guts which reminded him, when the bell sounded at noon, of the crying of his only child, stricken with measles, and beaten by the little chosen ones of the Lord because he'd never been baptised. Every day at noon, Dinombien heard his son crying at the gate of heaven. Dorismé spoke to him. And they went off to see Wet-Back. That evening as he came home to his little hut, Dinombien smiled at his woman. She was astonished:

—They raise you pay, Nombien?

—No, but I feel good, I don't know why.

All the long years they had lived together, Dinombien's wife had accepted his sudden bad moods when he came from work. She loved him, rough as he was. She couldn't understand this smiling man. She told the neighbours her man had gone out of his mind.

A change had come over Dinombien. But the old fellow was still sad when, on the stroke of noon, he heard his little son crying outside the gate of heaven.

It was Holy Water Saturday.

Vivi was coming through the slum, arms open wide, dancing on two wooden stilt legs up there above the crowd, all tumbling together down the slopes of Death's-Door. A great big Carnival figure, a cloth doll sewn up, tied up, daubed with paint, stuffed with straw, decked with caper flowers and crown-of-thorns. Arms outspread in a cross, she was coming, she was coming, wild with excitement the people whooped and yelled. Up there on Death's-Door they had dug up the skeleton of the old hag buried for years in the ground. And it was with her leg bones and her foot bones that they were beating the short sharp calling *kata* beat, and juggling the twisty reeds, spinning like propellers in their hands.

The people had opened their windows and doors, climbed up on the roofs and in the trees, and they threw down jug water and strong white rum on the grinning *Vivi* mask. It was clothed in a grotesque long white dress, some rich lady's négligée which the ravenous mob had taken from a sea front store one time of hysterical looting when they had descended on the town. The booty had been stored in an old wardrobe for a marriage that never happened. Nibbled by the termites and the rats, it was given as a dress for the doll, on this day when the witch's spell was finally to be broken.

Arms outspread in a cross, the doll danced on, and the people sang:

Sleep na, Vivi, bundle on yu back...

The small shopkeepers had closed their doors. Blindmen with faces blackened by the sun, beggars with dirty beards, women with drooping breasts: the crowd surged down the narrow street like an earthquake, calling aloud on the sun to cook the dug-up bones of the old hag. The sick people, some shaking with marsh fever, some yellow with cholera, some pale with infected sores, some agitated by mysterious fits, were carried on shoulders or crude wooden stretchers; for they believed that this was the day they would be cured. At every street corner, people were beating on the electric light poles, which resounded like the tolling bell of judgement day.

Decked in caper flowers and crown-of-thorns, *Vivi* danced on. And her ghastly grinning made the people nervous. Young boys riding donkeys with skinny legs scattered rose laurel flowers at the feet of girls who stood in their doorways watching the excited throng go by. Some picked up the flowers from the dust beside their bare toes, and fixed them on the sheets which had been stretched across walls by the old women as if it were Corpus Christi.

In each district the dense crowd was reinforced by a flood of ragged people, who came yelling out of the lanes and huts as if someone had opened cages full of starving slaves.

Vivi went right through the slum, carried along by the song.

The sky was low. At each crossroads where the doll appeared, a great shout rose up and then clouds of dust and clanging metal sounds. At the foot of Death's-Door, from the seething lanes to the far end of every dead-end alley, people shouted and made noise with sticks, kitchen knives, cobblers' cutters, tin-smiths' hammers, heavy iron bars, when up there above the old rusty roofs they saw the outline of the cloth doll wearing her transparent white silk négligée nibbled by the termites and the rats.

She would be sacrificed at noon.

Some had brought mortar-sticks that they held at arm's length like heavy clubs. Others clapped their hands. At the head of the crowd, the stalwart mosquito-hunters held *Vivi* firmly on their gleaming shoulders and were singing a nine-night *libera* tune with erotic swaying of hips. The figure had been so copiously sprinkled with strong white rum and jug water that long drips trickled from her open legs on to the crowd, who exclaimed in disgust at the idea that *Vivi* was making water on the shaven heads of the mosquito-hunters.

The people took over the lanes and the passageways like an earthquake, making the shack walls creak and singing amid the dust and the sun:

Sleep na, Vivi, bundle on yu back...

The old sun burned away. A smell of soot and sweat took over the air like the breath of a slaughtered beast. Moving together to the diabolical rhythm, the crowd went by. The sick people yellow with cholera, the lame ones carried on worn old canvas stretchers pissed and dribbled in an exhausted daze. The blind wept as they strove to imagine the colourful scene.

The children had heard so much about her evil ways and wicked deeds in the stories they had been told, that they were scared to come out of their huts and look at *Vivi*. They clung to the doors, hid under old iron beds or sheltered under their mothers' patched skirts. The men hauled them out forcibly, and they screamed themselves hoarse at the sight of the cloth doll with her painted-on teeth and open arms, piddling on the crowd in a flimsy dress. The folk who lived on the top of Death's-Door told how they often heard wailing and moans which set off the dogs barking at noonday. Just at the very spot where the body had been hung on the door, under the shack-shack tree, itself now a skeleton of dry branches.

The people had decided to put her to death a second time.

The date hadn't been chosen by chance. It was after the old hag's body had been buried three years, two months, three weeks and four days under the leafless shack-shack tree, under the burning sun on the top of Death's-Door. This was the duration of the great drought before the seven days and seven nights of rain. They had decided to dig up her old bones, resurrect her in the guise of *Vivi*, and then exorcise her spirit when the day reached its zenith.

Arms outspread in a cross, *Vivi* gave a ghastly smile.

Noon, cleansing away sins, word of the entrails, heart of night at the apex of day, voice of the child shut out of heaven, Baron Samedi sounding his bells and his anklets, had not yet struck.

Weariness of the town. Midday struck.

Vivi had disappeared.

All that was left was a big bonfire at the centre of the crossroads, kindled by the crowd clapping their hands. A great noon bonfire to force open the gates of heaven for the children shut out of paradise.

The caper flowers were burnt.

The bones were thrown into the flames.

The excitement died away in blackened ashes. In the distance a donkey brayed. The smoking pyre rose up towards the sun.

Three years I have wandered in search of you. I left my dwelling of stars and moons to follow you through the dust. I left my lotus garden to weep along your path. You never turned around to see me. Why do you not hear me when I call? See, over there, that path sown with diamonds, rubies and perfume. That is the way you will go if you give me back my golden comb. Over there, there is a mansion with satin curtains at its casements. You can open them to talk to the stars. You can close them if the moon comes a-courting through the panes. All that world of lights will be yours. Yours alone. You will live in purity and know no season.

Three years I have offered you all the gold in the sky and the sea in return for the comb stolen from the river while I bathed. Do you see what has happened to me? I am taking off my clothes so that you can see the piece of linen stained with blood. And my legs. These legs which have grown in place of my fish-tail since the day I lost my comb. Do you see. Blood and legs. Painful legs following you through the dust. And this blood that won't stop flowing. I have lost my virginity and been driven out of the Great Pool of the Triple Moon. To return there I must have the comb. I live behind the damp wall of the fountain. And I suck the water from the bricks. Today I shall stop the flow of the fountain so that you will come all alone, at midday I beg you, and give me back my comb. You will find a pot of gold. I've brought it, it's for you. All for you. I'll wait for you, remember, at midday, behind the fountain wall. All the riches in the world will be yours....

She had spent all the morning sewing a new dress, with her memory full of the Wanderer she had dreamt about at dawn. Each time she took a stitch she could see the beautiful white woman with the blue dress hanging down in tatters. Her monthly blood had flowed all through the night. She had put clean cloth into her panty. She was sitting, fresh and radiant, with her black hair hanging down over the back of the little chair. She remembered the time of the great drought. She had gone to the fountain to speak to the Wanderer because she couldn't bear to see men collapsing in the dust, or hear the dogs mournfully barking up at the sun. She had gone to see her at midday, to make the rain fall in exchange for the comb. The rain had come. It had swallowed up the homes and the people and washed away their animals.

She waited for midday.

The fountain was crowded with girls and boys, noisy with rattling of pails, curses and stamping of feet, bursting out in the sunlight like corn popping on the fire. The hollow sound of aluminum containers against the sides of the damp wall echoed like the rock landing on the old hag, the day they stoned her dead body, crucified up there on Death's-Door. When the water dried up in the pipe, only two little girls were left by the fountain, soaked from head to toe, but without a drop of water in their pails. They didn't want to go home to their parents for fear of a scolding. They turned the tap this way and that; it worked badly and grated with a sad metallic sound. Then they heard another noise, which at first they thought was the metal of the old broken tap. The noise went on, even when they had stopped touching the tap, coming closer like a jangling of hard things. The jangling bell-sound grew louder and louder behind the fountain wall. A long shuddering took hold of them and they fled away down the main path, feet in the dust and hair rising up to the sun, leaving their pails behind at the fountain edge.

The people were still lurking in their shacks, sheltering from the heat of the sun. The main path was silent. Only some flocks of pigeons flew around among the roof-tops or alighted somewhere in search of seeds.

At the stroke of twelve, in the middle of the road appeared the brown girl with her long plaits, as if in a ghostly dream. Her hair moved in the wind and her white dress trailed in a cloud of dust. Ten pigeons flew up from under her feet when she came to the crossroads, in the sight of the fountain. She saw not one but two pots shining in the glare of the sun.

One of them was overturned.

When with beating heart the long-haired girl drew near the fountain, she first turned on the tap and drank great gulps of cold water. And as she slaked her thirst, behind the wall she heard hard things jangling together like new coins.

And the beautiful woman appeared in her tattered blue dress.

— Look. The fine pots are for you. Riches. Thank you for coming to meet me. Tell me, how can you live here in the dirt and the dust, among the thieves and the filth? You should leave this world of rottenness, it's not the place for you. Nothing here is in your image. These men are not your brothers. They are false, vicious, foolish and rough. All the gold is for you alone. I want you to live in a realm of purity and ease. Set down the comb on the wall and you'll see. You'll see.

The comb trembled in her hand.

The two pots shone in the sun. One of them was overturned.

— I know today you have had your period. You still have blood on your white dress because you are keeping the comb. Give it back to me, I beg you! I have been asking you for it for three years, sucking the water out of the old wall so as not to die in the sun in this world of men. Give it back to me and put an end to my suffering. Set me free from these heavy legs and this blood that drains my strength. I beg you!

The comb trembled in her hand.

The two pots shone in the sun. One of them was overturned.

A long teardrop slid down the cheek of the Wanderer. Her face was infinitely sad and plaintive, behind the fountain wall. The long-haired girl bent down as if to touch the pots of gold.

— No! I beg you! Give me back the comb. First leave it on the wall. Give it back to me!...

She gripped the comb tightly in her hand.

The two pots shone in the sun. One of them was overturned.

She touched one pot. Suddenly both of them changed back into ordinary pails of beaten aluminum. Left behind by the two frightened little girls when they ran away. The jangling sound had stopped.

Perfectly calm, the long-haired brown girl went back home with the comb to take up her sewing, trying not to hear the sad wail of the Wanderer behind the fountain wall. With her hair falling down the back of the little chair, she gazed at the picture of the Virgin ascending into heaven, which was pasted up with starch on the wall of the shack above the clothes press.

She did not think of her own tears at leaving her place of birth, nor the sad bray of Breakback, the old donkey, when the black, fish-smelling man had taken the animal's rope. He had given her father forty gourdes as they waited for the truck going to town. Nor did she remember how her heart quailed like a frightened animal when the market crowd closed around the donkey—with their smell of salt herring and soap, their big straw hats to keep off the sun.

But she did remember her mother, so sad, poor woman, at leaving her patch of native soil, that as soon as she had got off the truck at the station, she had bought from a stall full of sashes, scapulars and candles, the picture of the Holy Virgin ascending into heaven. She put it into the bundle on which she rested her head under an arcade when rain fell, or carried on her shoulder, following behind her man as he searched for a plot of land to put up his hut. The girl had never looked on the Virgin before with so much admiration. And for the first time she believed that the Wanderer was with her in the room, so much did she resemble the Bride of Heaven. The same white skin. The same starry brightness. The same trail of hazy dreams. The same crescent moon. The same shower of heavenly jewels.

She stared a long time at the Virgin ascending into heaven, then went back to her sewing, her hair falling down the back of the chair. Its worn joints gave little creaks, like an old woman complaining to herself at the pain in her bones.

Using the rope that went over his shoulders, the man was dragging firewood in a box the shape of a coffin. In a cloud of heat and flies, beggars were resting in the shadow of the huts. Some slept or dreamed of sad things, speaking in their dreams or wetting their patched trousers. Women cared for their infants who, swaddled in old bits of flannel, suckled flat breasts hanging down on bony chests.

The man walked down the centre of the main track with the wood-box, which made a noise on the stones, annoying the dogs and rousing a blindman.

— What pig is that, eeeh! grunting in my sleep?

The blindman slashed at the air with his crooked stick. It was hot as an oven. The flies buzzed. The wood-box raised up dust in the middle of the path. Those who could see nudged the blindman to hold his peace.

— What pig is that, eeeh!... he went on.

The man had gone up to the blindman and caught a blow from the stick in his back. The noise stopped.

— Pig quiet now, said the wood-box man.

— Yes, mek him keep quiet. I hate pig for true. One time I had a pig, but I slit him belly with a spike because he pissed on me rags. I could a eaten it. I was hungry. But pig disgust me. I left his meat for the ants. Must kill all the pigs. Them animal eat they own shit!...

The wood-box man caught him by the collar.

— Eh! What is this? I hate pig meself. Smell too bad. Shitty beasts, pigs!

The man dragged the blindman out into the sun, and his eyelids trembled in the strong light. Some of the others took fright and watched with their lips quivering like idiots. Others were still deep in dreams of a bitch delivered of fifteen puppy-dogs, or a white hen shedding her feathers on a dried-up old calabash tree.

Once in the middle of the lane, they stopped.

— Tell me the story of the stuck pig!

— Well, you see, this pig he was stinking for true. All the time him grunting, and he wet up me rags with his piss that stink of Beelzebub. A whole week I spread those rags out in the sun, the time when no rain no fall. That devilish water wouldn't go away. So I make up me mind to take him to that gully where man and beast get drowned when it rain. Pig feel sad. Him grunt. And I stick him with the spike and let out all him gut down into the dust with the ant and the fly them. If I did still have me eyes, I would o' kill all the pig in this country. So...

Then a click clack. The blindman felt something through his guts, a feeling like an empty belly. Then he felt as if all his strength had ebbed away. He felt breeze blowing through his belly. He put up his hand to grope for the crooked stick, but collapsed into the blood-stained box without a sound.

The man turned away with a grimace, leaving the body in its coffin out in the burning sun. Once he had disappeared into a passageway, the beggars crept out of the shade and left that ill-fated spot with a clatter of sticks, crutches and bowls.

For more than a month now, since he'd been carried off to the little white house of the trinket-seller, Raphael had only left the mint-scented room the day he'd been taken to hospital. Plenty of people came to see him. The fat higgler on the corner told John to get the cards read. The woman whose husband had been killed in Cuba was now a Protestant convert, and came to pray at his hospital bed. Dormélia the laundress often dropped in during the day. Father Leon too, despite the weariness in his old limbs, came to chat about how his pigeons were straying and how corn was scarce.

When he got over the measles and got his strength back, Raphael could go and watch the television.

Television had come to the shantytown, with a noise of loudspeakers and sirens, drumming on old crates, raucous war-whoops, received with dazed stupefaction and wonder by a ragged population avid to see the peep-show of modern times.

An uproarious procession of shouting and dust had followed the mechanical Lady of Miracles to the place where a little altar of planks and tree branches had been set up. Two men climbed up on it. The white man spoke the language heard in the mouths of the men in the big sheds. The other was a trained black who translated into the language of the yards, the markets and the cockpits. Thus they came to know what the white man said. He said to control the births, they must space them out. Which wasn't easy to make people understand. So they showed it on the television: a picture of a mother feeding her baby. The people felt happy but bewildered, like little children looking in a mirror. Some even thought it was a vision, and went off home with their heads down, talking in strange tongues. Others said the woman resembled Saint Rose of Lima behind the glass window in her chapel. But then others protested, saying that saints never had bare breasts like our own women.

That evening, the heads of families met together. And they spoke of the light of the candle that must never go out.

That same night, they sent out men from the crest of Death's-Door to the new quarter by way of Seven-Dagger-Cut, and from Sorrow-Alley to the old Pig-Wallow, men to knock on the doors and wake up all the people sleeping in the starlight, spreading the message that, in spite of disease and the old sun, the race must not die out.

When they came for the eighth time to speak about birth control, they found a great mob of children, some naked, some with their shirts open down to their swollen belly-buttons, and only wanting to see the television pictures. They clamoured to see, with shouting and beating of saucepans, drowning the voice of the white man as he summoned the men and women who would not shake off their intimacies of breast and bone, nor disturb their sweaty sleep, for there they glimpsed in dreams things sad and hidden.

From that day forth, the number of births increased so fast that there were not enough stars in the sky to watch over all the Christian souls. One day, the good Lord was astonished at the great increase in his flock. One night when the heavy snoring of the sleepers had driven away the clouds, a great shower of comets descended on the earth like brides on a vast migration. A few days later, some fifteen children were dead, all stricken by the marsh fever. Their stars had come to carry them off, so people said.

And so it was a time of deep mourning. And the people blamed the intruders who had come with the picture peep-show, and given out pills to swallow that must have poisoned the children. And so they received them with a volley of stones. They didn't have a chance to give their last speech. They came once more, but this time with a truckload of police, to teach a proper respect for the dignity of Science. There were beatings and more pills were given out.

Raphael had heard the painful sound the gun butts made as they hit against ribs and skulls. He had seen people groan, blindmen run, mothers cradle their children between their breasts in vain to protect them. He asked Father Leon why the police had entered into the business of birth control. The old man told him some history, recounting the beatings in front of the big sheds fifteen years before. John too had told Raphael of the day when the gunman, in a fit of blue fever, had injured his passengers. It all left him with a bitterness at heart. Why some people them can beat and give licks, but other people is only suffer them suffer?

And one day he was with some boys carrying slingshots who hung out at the corner. He hit on the head an armed man who was chatting with a prostitute. The boys sped away down the alleys before anyone could see.

Ever since the long pond of stinking mud had been dried out, the area cleared of dung that polluted it, the evenings filled with woodsmoke to drive off the mosquitoes, and people stopped from relieving themselves every here and there, the rose laurels grew in front of the whitewashed cottages and only one pigeon had been buried with the kitchen knife. In spite of rains, the dead light of moons and terrible dog days, the Flower-Town quarter kept the whiteness of its old walls and the colour of its dust.

So too the old people, warming themselves silently in the sun on their wicker chairs, kept repeating past gestures, from when the huts first began to spring up along the edge of the long pond of stinking mud. This man is pulling something like a thread out of the clouds, and scarcely remembers that as a little naked boy he loved to launch bright paper kites up into the clear sky. That man, standing in front of his old crooked door, mouth gaping and eyes glazed, is waving goodbye. Yet he has forgotten all those people who left: his mother, he had watched her going off with her bundle down the sandy path in the dry river bed, walking behind the old donkey whose infected sore drew flies: she never came back. His father, who left with his machete strung over his shoulders to look for the woman who hadn't come back; he didn't come back either. His cousins (the country is so small everyone believes they're the same family), valiant country folk who all down the years have taken to the road. And he too set out, toes in the dust, with his pregnant wife who was to give him three babies at once in the first slum that took them in; the woman he was to bury when she caught the marsh fever, and then one of his brave sons, who'd gone out armed with a pickaxe to struggle with the others against the water on the fourth day of the flood, and had been swallowed up by the mouth of the drain with terrible screams. And then the other two who left for Santo Domingo to cut cane or hump bananas: he'd never had news of them.

Every day in the sun and the dust, standing by his crooked door, he waves goodbye, mouth gaping and eyes glazed, to all those sad journeys man makes against his will.

The dispossessed still came with their dreams which glided over the city from one gate to the other ....

They came from so far they were weary. They went to sleep at the edge of the big cemetery with their children, breast to breast, leaning against the white walls. Stacked up like heaps of dead bones, they had no morbid dreams. They just wanted to smell the freshness of the white walls and watch the shooting stars over the graves. The police came and forced them to move on. His Excellency the President of the Republic must not see the sad colour of their teeth or the length of their nails. They were shoved along with truncheon blows and, scraping the walls, they dug their nails into the newly painted masonry, wanting to carry away with them this white dust that had lured them, and the memory of the comets. Bones, whiskers, teeth and bundles, they hit against each other without a groan, one leaning on a shoulder, another limping on wounded legs. The dogs saw them coming in the last grey days of October. On hot evenings, attracted by the strong smell coming from the edge of the cemetery, they came to sniff these bodies lying rolled up in old sacking under the stars. The poor people had tamed the dogs, and they left together when the police drove them away. Destined to live together, they belong to the same race. The lost people collapsed like disjointed puppets near the white walls of the Flower-Town quarter, and the dogs they had brought with them kept watch besides their masters' bodies, barking at the sun.

A season of sadness was coming, and perhaps because of that, the rose laurels flourished. They covered roofs, curled in at windows and sprouted under tables or in the straw of chairs. No sooner pruned back, their branches sprang up again, and it took effort to get out of the cottage doors. The flowers grew with such vigour and so abundantly that they spread to other sections of the slum and also invaded the hut windows and roofs. You went to sleep one day in an old board house and woke up next morning in a bower of blossom and branches. The lost people were amazed by this frantic plant life which they couldn't explain.

Raphael went to look for Father Leon, whom he hadn't seen for a week because of the Festival of Flowers, and he found the door blocked with branches. It took hours to clear away, and when he got into the room, to his amazement all he could see was the rocking chair Father Leon used to bask in the sun. It was held prisoner by many branches that clung to the old wooden frame like twining *lianas*. The old priest was no more. All that was left of him was his stick and a pair of worn shoes in front of the chair. Silent, dusty. He had died there in his rocking chair the day before the rose laurels had begun their invasion. Drawn in by his decomposing smell, the plants had transformed his bones into the branches that stretched over the roofs. Clusters of pink flowers bloomed on the wooden chair, in the pale sunlight filtering through the open window.

The ghetto children stopped their games: one of them had been beaten till the blood ran for singing a song that was forbidden. Why were people so vexed? All they wanted to do was celebrate the marvellous explosion of rose laurels. One of them, innocent and bold, went down the path singing: "Little rose-bush climb so high, climb up high de little rose; stepmama she not yu mama." The child was battered down like an animal. He was only ten years old. His mother went mad.

The frenzy of the rose laurels brought on a great epidemic of blue fever. It spread from the old Pig-Wallow to the area of the last remaining marshes, skirting round the thick walls of the big sheds.

Dinombien's old shoes still trod the familiar road leading to the *Incorrperaytid*. His wife thought her man must be bewitched. But Dinombien himself was standing up taller than ever before.

Down the main way came a woman with two children on her shoulders and ten or so others, all skinny and bare. This little flock had come from the farthest slum where they had killed the children for singing the flower song. They trailed along in the dust, bang-bellies, stick legs, desperate eyes and penises dangling dismally down. For a week now they had been walking, searching for a new land. The Virgin had appeared to the woman, telling her to make up her bundle and leave with her children. She'd managed to collect a score of them, and on the way had sold six in the market to people who said they needed them and now here she was with the others in the sad blue light of morning.

Gathering up courage, with the Virgin their guide, fleeing the blue fever, the little flock in every place it passed retied the grimy knot of its bundle. Eternal wanderers, searching for a new land. The woman with her nipples hanging down to her belly told that wherever she went, she ran from death. That at every open door, she begged for bread and water. That all over the ancient ruins and wild thickets of old Fort Mercredi, clusters of pink flowers had suddenly sprouted. That children were attacked and pitilessly beaten, just for singing about it. So they responded with the story of the woman gone mad, and showed her the rose laurels over the roofs. Then she retied the knot of her bundle, and with a pathetic shuffling of bang-bellies, stick legs, and dangling penises, they all trailed away towards the dusk.

Under the burning sun, the big grey sheds glared horribly. Though it had been there for so many years, *Incorrperaytid* remained a mystery to the dispossessed, as the monster spread its tentacles wider to combat the attack of flowers. The lost people watched as steel fangs, iron caterpillar tracks, smoking phallus and bestial growling crushed their shacks like cardboard. The greater part of the cleared space was reserved for the big men of the sheds. On what was left other buildings were put up, where every morning crowds waited for work. Pushed around by surveyors, new landowners, magistrates and gun butts, thirty men waited on two yards of ground, suffocating, tormented by flies, mosquitoes and mud. At first they screamed like mad people. At night you could hear their groans like slaughtered beasts as far away as the bottom of I-believe-in-God alley. Then they flung rocks against the walls to show their anger. The police, with blows as usual, demanded they keep quiet.

But their silence was more ominous than screams, and the frightened men of the sheds armed a night-watchman at the main gate to safeguard the property. Two days later, when the HASCO siren sounded, they found the watchman's body mutilated by knives. There was a sign on him with these two words, which not everyone could understand: *Traitor, Antinational*.

At the centre of town, fear took on nightmare colours. In the surrounding slums—down alleys narrower then the crack between two fingers—came a terrible season without winds, stars, rain or butterflies, just dry as an old carcass or a broken chair.

The guards had come.

They came through the doors, smashed in the windows, kicked down the masonry of old walls, herded the women outside, pushed the children, hit the men, tore up holy pictures, wounding anyone who resisted, raping the prettiest girls, and setting fire to whole densely-packed blocks. The kids howled. The women screamed. The men kept silent.

There were about a hundred of them. They gave short orders. They carried rifles.

They had backed the crowd up against the shack walls, with their hands behind their heads. You could hear the people's breath like a bull ruminating.

They shouted at the people, demanding a definition of the word *Antinational* found on the watchman's body. Silent, the people only made answer with their heavy animal breathing. So they pulled three boys out of the crowd. They trained their gun barrels on the backs of their young necks. The guards made it known that they would blow their brains out at the least sign of revolt. Cold metal behind his sweating neck, his bare dusty feet beside the huge muddy boots; big tears rolled down Raphael's cheeks as he thought of his father with the old bus. Headbones, fossillised skulls, old men's whiskers, penises shrunk between their balls, feet rooted in the dust: the lost people looked at their children.

— *Antinational?*

The echo died away right over at I-believe-in-God alley. Silence was the only answer.

Suddenly a voice shouted out:

— *TRAITORS! MURDERERS!*

In the middle of the ragged throng, a man raised his fist, shouted out his anger. He was not afraid to show it in spite of their guns.

They hauled him brutally out of the crowd, away from the bony fingers like protective roots stretched out towards him. His clothing tattered, his anger frothing on his lips, the man was shoved savagely against the remaining wall of a broken shack, facing the others.

With their guns trained on his chest, the guards ordered him to define *Antinational*. Instead he spat out his anger. He said that death didn't frighten him, that he didn't have the head of a judas who for a few gourdes would hand over his blood brother, that no words could tell of the suffering of his comrades; that....

— See them! See them there! They come knock on your gate because them hungry. You did spit in they face, push them down in the swamp dirt. Shame you give them. Them is animal, you know, because them don't know how to answer when you cuss them! Them is animal because you a kill them pickney and they don't know how to bawl! When we can't even bury we pickney when them dead from hungry, is what we look like to the foreigners? Like slave! *Antinational* is people like you now, with your big guns, stopping the children of this country from living on they own land!...

A young guard, with tears in his eyes, threw down his rifle, and ran over to the crowd shouting "Power to the people! Power!" A hail of bullets tore through his back. He fell down in the dust.

— *MURDERERS!* the people turned.

At the same instant a volley hit the angry man. Soaked in blood, he still had the courage to give one more shout before he fell heavily, chest upward and nails embedded like claws in the mud bricks of the ruined hut.

Midday sounded. But he couldn't hear, one last time, his little boy crying outside the gates of heaven. Dinombien's body lay in the dirt.

Then the ragged mob pressed forward, in spite of the threat of the guns. They were ordered back. The tide of men came forward, silently, heavily, big hands by their knees. The gun shots rang out again. The men kept on coming. Heavily. Stepping over bodies soaked in blood. A third time the guns fired. At that moment out of the crowd, amid the dead bodies of men, pregnant women, the dust, blood, sun and gunfire, came the beautiful long-haired brown girl, dazzling in her white dress. With arms wide open and begging for mercy, she knelt before the big muddy boots of the man shouting orders. Her hair fell down in the dust beside the thick boot soles and she begged the man to stop the shooting. The martyred crowd, at the sight of the beautiful brown girl all in white, thought that the Virgin Mary had miraculously appeared and fell back with the guns still trained upon them.

The shooting stopped.

The man who gave orders pulled back the head of the young girl, unable to understand her magic, stronger than guns, for turning a people back. With his two legs firmly astride, the man now grew disturbed, looking into the eyes of the beautiful brown girl who knelt before his huge form. He had never seen a being of such beauty. In the midst of this orgy of blood, groans, blue sunlight, gunpowder and dust, the young girl's shining eyes submerged cruel reality and his crime in a dream of stars beyond time. The man standing, legs astride, stared fixedly at the tearful eyes, the outstretched arms, the trailing hair, the faint contour of breasts and the whiteness of her dress.

Monumentally anchored in his two boots with the pleading girl before him like a wounded dove, the man felt himself transforming into a cathedral.

Up through his body of quivering stone he could feel the rising processions of men doomed to be shot at dawn.

Up through his flesh of quivering stone he could feel rising the moans from torture chambers.

Up through his veins of quivering stone he could feel a rising surge of bank vault smells and factory smoke.

Up through his bones of quivering stone rose orgies of moons, rivers and birds. Then the man-cathedral closed his eyes to shut in this life-force inhabiting him. And he could feel descending wave upon wave of condemned men, bank vault smells, moons turning out of control in revolution.

And the cathedral, its structure now unsupported, collapsed.

As he lay in the dust before the beautiful brown girl, the colonel's fly was stained. He came back from a timeless dream and a journey among the stars giving off a strong smell of gunpowder and semen.

Like a huge eye appalled at the sight, the old sun rose over the dead. He had knocked around the hill-tops up on Death's-Door, disappearing at the narrow opening of I-believe-in-God alley before he shone right down into Jesus-Grave, the name that had eventually been given to the deep crevasse carved out by the falling thunder-stone on the sixth day of the great rains. The wind blew away the dust and smoke of the burnt-out shacks with their odour of sacrifice. No more groaning. No more wailing could be heard. Only the whistling of the sea breeze which blew down the deserted lanes and the silent passageways, pushing open a window shutter or lifting a corner of the tattered rags covering a corpse to expose to the sun its chest punctured with red holes. Beyond the melancholy barking of dogs and the braying donkeys which occasionally broke the silence, beyond the smoke and the mounds of blackened earth, the city seemed to sleep at the feet of the slum, crowned by the cathedral towers in the dignity of their everlasting stone.

She didn't know how she had got out. The dispossessed had all taken fright. They had stayed hidden among the smoking ruins like hermits, their eyes staring. All covered in dust, like a lifeless bundle, she had emerged from her hole. She walked down the deserted main path the way a lost one never walks, that is with head bent and eyes full of tears.

She dragged herself to the edge of Jesus-Grave.... There she sank to her knees, mouth gaping. The body which lay on the ground was spoiled like a tomato. Then a terrible shuddering took hold of her; she raised her arms to heaven. She opened her mouth, moved her lower jaw: no words came out. Speechless, wild-eyed, this poor huddle of flesh could see only processions passing of faceless men armed with whips, priests in black cassocks, trolleys loaded with coffins, full of sad jangling bells, and a beast that unfurled its vast black wings, proud and warlike.

She wanted to scream. No words came. Numbly they piled one upon the other like zombies.

Midday sounded.

It was then, for the first time, she too heard her little son, Cépremier, crying at the gate of heaven.

And then the words tumbled out of her throat:

— Cépremier!... Cépremier, me son! They take off Nombien skin! They skin him like a pig!

The child at the gate of heaven cried louder than ever.

The woman screamed with a superhuman power as if she would cough up her lungs. Blood came from the corners of her lips.

— Cépremier, me son! They skin him like a pig! Woi! me son! Woi! Me head like a coffin....

Midday passed with the sad voice of the little boy at the gate of heaven.

She had lost her voice again, and was shaken by shuddering fits. She ground her yellowed teeth. Then bit deep into the battered flesh of her husband's corpse, in the chest as if she wanted to devour his uncorrupted heart. But her teeth were blocked by the ribs. She rose to her feet, her face smeared with blood, and disappeared once again among the smoking ruins, a beast looking for its hole.

The bodies rotted as the days went on, and the sun didn't stop the terrible stench from spreading over the ruins. Plague breathed over all. Travelled along the rose laurel branches. Reached where the doves were perching. And increased the population of mosquitoes and flies.

Then the lost people, with the faces of men on the run, crept out of their lairs. They went hurriedly towards the corpses, dragged them along in the dust and heaved them into the depths of Jesus-Grave.

The appalling remains of Dinombien came to lie, by some mysterious means, at the entrance to the guardpost of the forces of Security and Order.

They'd arrived one morning with their tough shoulders and their cursing and settled into wooden barracks—once an old storehouse. They painted it yellow and hung up a flag on a pole. The signboard written up on the newly painted front identified their section, and the large portrait placed just opposite the door of the main room proved their unswerving devotion to the President of the Republic and to "Forward the Revolution".

The man who had gone around with the fire-wood box was appointed head of this section. Bramoulé Kandjolus had given up his trade as embalmer to become second-in-command. They controlled ten or more henchmen who spent their time between domino games on the porch, the rum bottle, the women attracted to them because they inspired fear, and keeping the uprooted in line.

They were the new papas of the ghetto.

Dinombien's stench woke them up very early. When they examined his remains, they found this inscription, which they couldn't understand:

> *Dis freedom body na go rot in de sun*
> *Gwine bear corn, gwine bear de blossom*
> *Right back to Guinea land.*

— Some traitor from the boats, they decided.

They stripped it with gusts of noisy laughter, and pissed all over it in their revellry. The ants began by covering the sores and rotten flesh. They moved into the sex, the eyes, mouth, nose. In a few hours the body was reduced to a

revolting heap of battered, half-eaten pieces with a decomposing stench which spread into their uniforms the colour of a stormy sea, their cartridge belts, the tables and even
into the fresh yellow paint on the walls of the new guardpost. Then just as mysteriously as they'd appeared, the stinking remnants of Dinombien vanished.

The stink of the corpse almost drove the guards mad, they
couldn't stand the smell in their clothes. The blame fell on
Dormelia, who did their laundry. They locked her up in
their makeshift prison, but when the walls began to ooze
with the stench, they had to fling the prison door open wide
and let in the sunlight. The sun shone and out of the door
with the old washerwoman marched an army of huge
cockroaches in a gloomy procession. They spent two whole
days washing down the guardpost walls. But Dinombien's
stench wouldn't go away. They'd started to batter the walls
with clubs, but after the first moment of wild rage,
remembered the big portrait of the President of the Republic
(a crude copy of the original) and let drop their weapons
for fear of disrespect to the sacred image of the nation's
Father.

As day followed day, weary, woebegone, powerless, they
eventually got used to the stench. And everywhere they
went, Dinombien went with them, sticking closer than their
shadow.

The guards had come with their tough shoulders to protect the spread of *Incorrperaytid*, and blue fever was
spreading too, like the end of the world. And yet the rootless
ones were still driven towards town by the same dry and
stricken wind, taking the same road no wider than a kitchen
door. The caterpillar tracks of the big sheds crushed to the
ground children and dreams as humble as that of owning
an old pair of shoes. Yet in spite of the echo of weeping
borne on the hot night wind, every day the dispossessed
thronged in front of the main gate to trade-in their hunger
and empty hands. The elders of Father Leon's generation,

warming themselves in the sun, said it had been the same when the 'mericans first set up their sugar domain, over there, where other shacks had been. They remembered a song from those days, one that used to make them wild enough to fling rocks:

> *Me come from down deh and me come up so*
> *When me reach by de Suga' fact'ry*
> *Can't talk oh! cause o'de pain*
> *Holy Virgin our mother is where you is?*
> *St. Francis our father is where you is?*
> *You lef you Bel-Air people a go lay de track for Suga'*
> *Can't talk oh! for de pain.*

Incorrperaytid stretched out its grasp. Where once the mosquito-hunters had built their fires, the tractors bared their fangs. An Arawak axe and links of rusty chain alike were unearthed there. But these things which could tell their past to the people were quickly ground back into the dust.

One of those full moon mornings that you see only over graveyards of shacks like these, the woman with the flock of children came back. People recognized her, and asked for news of one of her boys, the one who used to trudge along reciting long verses while endlessly peeing along the road: he had met his death on the sidewalk by the white walls of the big cemetery in town. It was only then she remembered that she had been here before, and how at the sight of the rose laurels she had gone off into the dusk. She had lost her memory for places, slums and alleyways. It really wasn't easy to tell them apart in this ill-fated season. The layer of dust in front of the shacks was the same thickness, the dogs howled the same way at the moonshine, the air stank with the same smell of death, there was the same old sun, and everywhere the same yellow barracks with the flag on top. The same curse hung over everything.

She was going from one place to the next with her sad little flock, looking for a new land. And yet, it was thanks to her that the most distant places were in contact with those closest at hand: All who suffered from the terrible blue fever soon came to value her madness and her eternal wandering. When she arrived in a district, people would greet her, calling her Walk-bout Woman, and there was always someone to add or rub out a *vèvè* sign or secret word in charcoal on the cloth of her bundle. She was never parted from that old sack, with its pots, papers, shoe heels and secret messages. One evening when they were resting, she said to the oldest of her flock, as she pointed up to heaven, that what was needed to feed all her little children scattered over the slums was to reap the moon, the most magical coin in the world. The child believed it, and every full moon he threw smooth round stones like eggs up at the clouds. Walk-bout Woman never gave up hoping for a marvellous harvest of moon.

A morning full of freshness and the croaking of frogs. In the vast rustling of leaves full of singing crickets, amid the powerful fragrance of leafmould made of dead birds, bark of ancient trees, river mud and star droppings, with the mud of the swamps drying on them up to the waists, stung by the mosquitoes, lashed by the fiercest rains, torn by the thornbush and scorched by the sun, they had reached the water's edge, fleeing from the machine gun fire and the tracker dogs of the *Guardia Nacional*. In the moment he spent looking at the tree blossoms drifting on the shining water, the man had some trouble recognizing the dead face of Dorillon who was making wild movements, as if trying to tell him about the darkness in the prostitute's room and the rope which tightened around his Adam's apple. Though he tried not to remember his fallen comrades, for at that particular moment every second counted, he had seen Cassagnol again rising out of the muddy swamp in a scarlet halo of flame-tree bloom. It was towards him that he dived with María Isabel's slipper, as they riddled her with bullets at the river's edge. Twice his 'paniard girl with the ripe corn skin had come towards the city, seeking out her man's house at the time of the reprisals and arrests. She had crossed over the border to tell him that they hadn't buried her, that her body had rotted by the riverside amid the star droppings, the vermin and the mouldering flesh of dead birds. The smell of her corpse blended into the smell of the other dead in the shanties.

The unquiet woman the colour of ripe corn floated through the squalid space on rainy afternoons as on pale mornings. Shadowy landscapes and memories passed through her head in long sad processions: she was a rough country girl who had learnt to make love to earn a living. After the death of her mother, the only person around her who hadn't died of fever, María Isabel had set out to take her chance. And as she knew no trade but sewing and there was no profit in that, she had gone in search of whore-money. It's true that she had been overwhelmed by a terrible need to vomit when she saw the endless tail of the short man offering her twenty pesos. She had spent a long time staring bashfully at this enormous thing and bawled like a foolish little girl. That was her first encounter with trading in pleasure. Of course she wasn't a virgin. From the age of sixteen she had slept with the son of a rich landowner on a big banana plantation. When the owner got to know about the trivial contacts between María Isabel and his son, he came several times to beat little María, and threw her mother and big brother off his property where they had been settled for many years. The brother had gone off to some other country and never came back. María Isabel, eventually used to her new life, stopped crying when faced with naked men with their tails too long or too short. At certain times of the year, she went devoutly to place flowers and candles at the feet of the Virgin of Altagracia in Hyguey province, as if to cleanse herself of her sins.

One day, several of her sisters in misfortune had crossed the border, hired by a dealer with experience trading in Spanish girls the colour of ripe corn. María Isabel couldn't cross to the other side of the island because she didn't have a pretty floral dress or a good pair of shoes. It was then she had begun to spend exhausting nights drinking and fondling the bodies of strangers, sneaking into the compound that held the cane cutters. When the man met her, in that hell where they slaved in the sun and died like flies, it was her superb breasts that first attracted him. Among those hunted, humiliated, spied on, he wasn't the only one to appreciate her charms. But he was the first to pronounce a word so rich in meaning that she had fully understood only when she'd seen the red blossom of the flame-of-the-forest on the water of the Pedernales on that morning of freshness and croaking of frogs. Freedom, that ideal dreamt of, sought for, lost again, she still dragged it along with her, all soiled by the thick layer of dust, as any dead woman's sandal would be. It had been a long interval of fleeing, of lights, of fossilized memories and painful partings.

At the thought of her man's persecuted life, grotesque figures sprang up before her: undertakers with herring boxes, torturers and criminals baring their teeth, ministers' jackets, silhouetted priests demanding a thanksgiving mass, judges' robes, all these distorted images rose up and faded in their ghostly landscape. She was determined in spite of it all to see again the man who had told her about freedom, the man whose right cheek had been slashed by the *capataces*, and on whose hairy chest she used to rest her warm feet.

The unquiet soul and Walk-bout Woman went through all the slums under the moon, under the stars, through graveyards, down passageways, past the yellow barracks with the flag on top. One with the memory of her shoe and her floral dress, the wind blowing through her body like an open window. The other with her tattered rags all haloed around with the dream of reaping the moon. In life as in death, the wanderings of the dispossessed lead always to the same destiny.

It was a moonless night. After visiting all the huts in I-believe-in-God alley and passing under the leafless shack-

shack tree up on Death's-Door, the unquiet soul of the ripe corn coloured woman dragged herself to the front of the yellow barracks and smelt the stench of death. So she went to visit the makeshift prison: in front of it, men who stank of dug-up corpse were laughing around a table. Among them, sitting on the fat legs of the wood-box man whose sneering laughter echoed right over the slum like a horse's neigh, she saw Theresa Nunez, one of her sisters in the trade who had managed to cross the border. She was caressing with her red-nailed fingers the huge bare belly of this man who had put on kilos of fat since he had been appointed boss of the section, and no longer dragged around with his coffin-like box in the dust. She was half-naked. Gleams of light from the kerosene lamp (the only one in the slum) danced over her yellow body, her navel deep as a bottle mouth, and down to her thighs which the man was fondling while his followers looked on. He was flashing dollar bills about, and Theresa Nunez gave a hysterical laugh, which was drowned by the horse-like neigh. The unquiet spirit floated through the wall adorned with the majestic portrait of the President of the Republic, and into the dungeon from which no one ever returned.

In the thick darkness faintly penetrated by a pale glimmer from the kerosene lamp, she saw heavy shapes of prostrate bodies, some moaning, others still as stone. Bony hands brushed away cockroaches. Once outside the gloomy den, certain that the man with the scarred right cheek was not in the cells, she couldn't see Theresa Nunez laughing like a guinea-hen, nor the man with the horse's neigh, nor his gaping henchmen. They had all vanished into thin air. Only the moans of the prisoners rose up like a broken symphony into the moonless night.

The unquiet woman the colour of ripe corn kept on seeking the man who spoke to her of freedom. Walk-bout Woman never gave up hoping for her marvellous harvest of moon. The Wanderer, hidden behind the damp fountain wall, felt her end approaching and utterly forgot the magic spells which haunted the dreams of the beautiful long-haired brown girl. The Wanderer began to grind her teeth. In spite of the vast inertia of the lost people, and the thick layer of dust in front of the shacks, and the dogs howling to the moon and the same death smell in the air, and the old sun, and the yellow barracks with the flag on top, what worried the Wanderer was her hair, which she was beginning to shed like falling leaves, a sign of unmistakeable aging: she who passed through seasons, ages and years without knowing their identity, held in a pool of brilliant light in whose radiance she was queen over the waves, directed the wind, controlled the tide and calmed the storms. That storm, muffled, inaudible and yet more terrifying than the rumbling of the water at the mouth of the drain; that was gathering in the slums in spite of the yellow barracks, coming from the stars in spite of the dust, fertilising new shoots of rose laurel with the corpse of Dinombien, that was the storm that would take some stopping.

On a sunny afternoon when weary porters snored and the newspaper vendor nodded, wrapped in the latest edition of the official press, its headline proclaiming: "Peace and order reign in the slums", through the sparkle of her pinch-beck trinkets, her multicoloured headties, royal-blue kerchiefs, red cloths in honour of Ogun, and her little vials of perfume, the mint-scented woman, who had hauled herself up on top of her stall, saw the bloody mouth of the woman who had devoured her own child.

The police wagon was forcing a way through the dense crowd, and through the barred openings you could see the tragic expression of she who had been found in a hut eating the cold bleeding fruit of her womb. The baying of the mob came like a distant echo, rising and falling.

For the first time in the shanties, a woman among the rootless ones, tortured by the terrible pangs of sickness, had forgotten the mythical hope that children represented. And it was because she had forgotten that sacred hope, that people shouted as the van went by: "Mek she burn in hell!"

Passiona hadn't shouted with the others but when the police wagon passed directly in front of her stall and she saw the bloodstained mouth, red as her squares for Ogun, she couldn't resist a terrible weight that overcame her from her head to her knees. She broke the planks of her display.

As she fell Passiona pulled her pinchbeck trinkets down with her, and her headties, her kerchiefs and all her glittering metallic wares. She hadn't been able to bear the animal violence of that look which penetrated people and things, mournful as an earth-tremor.

A few days later, everyone heard that the woman had died in jail. Glad that their curses had struck her down even in her prison cell, the lost people looked up at the sun that afternoon, seeing something pathetic, as if they saw the woman burning in its fiery rays. Passiona was the only person to close her doors and windows, and remote from the sounds of the outside world, she let her breasts be sucked by the man wild with love because of the mint scent under her arms. She didn't have to leave the door half-open to wait for him any more. They made love quite naked the first time in the mint-scented room. Passiona breathed in the animal smell of his torso stinking of engine fumes. And twined together, they went on dreaming all day long, until they were disturbed in the evening by the horse-like neigh vibrating over the ghetto. It was then that John made to Passiona the most significant observation of his whole life as a lost one:

— That beast in the yellow barracks come here fe help the shed men bulldoze we home and we rose-bush!

It had taken him a good time to arrive at this truth.

Since the time of the reprisals and Dinombien's death, since that hard day when in place of his shack all he saw was a heap of dirt and boards, John had begun to ask himself questions about events which until then he had endured as inevitable blows of fate. The long day spent with Passiona had been enough to bring out of him, liberated a little by the fantasies and obsessions of this woman smelling of mint, that spark of genius which made him one more of the dispossessed ready to emerge from the shadows.

As they welled up in his memory, he tried to reconstruct the landscapes, dead or dusty, burnt or stained with blood:

the daily world of need, plague and blue fever which invaded the slums like a cancerous wind. He saw again the man in a hurry who asked for three thousand gourdes in exchange for the old Ford, and left him with a crate that could do nothing but scrape along the city avenues. He saw again the fetid pond where those hardy pioneers the mosquito-hunters had struggled for long months against the mud to put up their little whitewashed cottages and plant the rose laurels they'd brought in their bundles. He hadn't forgotten the blood on the mouth of the woman whose husband had been beheaded in Cuba, or the day when the lost ones marched out to burn the bodies at the mouth of the drain. He hadn't forgotten that heap of dirt and boards on the site of his shack, nor the first evening when he heard the horse's neigh, that neigh which was still vibrating and frightened the children who knew it was the devil's laugh. He forgot Madeleine who'd left him for the sake of five hundred gourdes, but thought of Raphael, who'd nearly had his brains blown out the day when the people had to define the word *Antinational*.

The word, which rang hollow in his memory or at least dimly, was to echo in his mind until the day when, in front of the cathedral in the tumult of the sublime apotheosis, he would see the beautiful long-haired brown girl, sitting in a little chair, sink deeper and deeper into the ground beneath the dusty rose laurels.

The sweat and mint smell of that long, passionate day didn't remind him of the sad time when he brewed himself potions with flowers and tree roots to restore the vigour of his limp tail. But there came images, slightly enlarged, of the enormously long flapping shoes worn by the drowned corpses, and the violent rush of people setting out to conjure away the plague smell.

When he heard the horse's neigh again, still wanting to convince Passiona, he reminded her of those nights cloudy with the mosquito-hunters' smoke, along that low-lying place of marshes. Now that place didn't belong to them, those fine men didn't own the cottages any more, their rose laurels couldn't grow in front of the doors. You had to pay big rent or they'd break up the place, fling you in jail, finish you off—and now it all belonged to the man in the yellow barracks over there.

— When the shed man want this land, he will put us down like dog, so he can feel their dollar in him pocket. He love the 'paniard gal them come from over the border to tickle him tail....

— So Missa Government don't love us at all. For him we come like dog, is that what you say, man?

Passiona, still simple as a girl, felt all confused and intimidated by this new blazing look appearing on John's brow. It would be five years before she felt again the violence of this look, as the huge crowd massed around the cathedral where the dusty rose laurels were blooming.

— Since the day we come to town we been nothing but dog! Those men in the big shed them take us for animal. That man in the yellow house....

— Missa Government?

— That same one! Him know well that we are pigs! Nothing but a herd of pig!

She felt herself possessed by the force of his anger. But when the horse's neigh came again, she thought the devil-man was at the window and she hid herself against John's chest. Then he gave in to his desire to challenge the guard with fierce and dreadful words. He noisily took down the shutter. Gleams of moonlight and the tune of the little boy's flute entered the dimly lit room full of the scent of mint. Through the open window, John shouted in a deep voice:

— Get yourself out of our moon, you dutty beast!....

Every pool of water would be poisoned if it mirrored a star. Every beggar's crutch would break if it pointed to the moon...Every door would be nailed up if it led to a path. But there were so many stars shining, so many moons waxing and waning, the paths were so long and dusty and full of sun that the waiting days grew stale as leafless trees. The crutches didn't fulfill the hope of pointing out the moon. Rusty iron latches held the doors closed. And the pools, to avoid reflecting the starry nights, filmed over with thick layers of mud and gave off an indefinable dead rat smell. Then in her impatience to recover her lost treasure, the Wanderer began feeling her bones crack. So with a sinister cracking of bones and the sadness of one risen from the grave, she appeared that day through the spiralling smoke of his fat cigar to Mister Longthread, he whose power extends from the sugar lands to the walls of *Incorrperaytid* via the strongrooms of banks in their airconditioned towers. She walked up and down his well-appointed room in such a frenzy that the sound of her bones set up a fearful vibration. The Wanderer had come from behind the oozing wall of the fountain to tell Mister Longthread her sorrow and how unbearably heavy were the legs that had grown from her torso. The anguish of losing her comb had changed her completely. Mister Longthread held sway from little farm plots to properties vast as the sky, embracing roads, villages, rivers. Enterprises like *Incorrperaytid*, squeezing the densely populated slums of the uprooted and growing fat like birds of prey. Also huge factories with phallocratic chimneys. The land he controlled didn't even stop where the great migration of doves had gone to die.

And as he had both cosmic imagination and promethean power, one day he felt the urge to bring into the world a marvel, and from one of his ribs he fashioned a woman, but not in his likeness. Yet she was the image transcending his heavy-fingered hands smelling of cigar smoke, the breath of his words that clouded the stars, and his walk like an ice-age monster, the grotesque, ancient carcass lashed by rain. This woman had hair hanging down to the dazzling fish-scales of her hips. She was white. They said she smelled of citronella and lemon balm, and that the perfume lingered over the river for hours after she bathed. So much talk of her, she became haloed with mysteries. Down she came into the yard of the whitewashed cottages as if mounted on a chariot of light. They called her Diamond-Rivermaid. The countryfolk and their children feared this beauty. They worshipped her. They muttered about the wickedness of the landowners, but they were dazzled by the radiance of the Diamond-Rivermaid.

So Mister Longthread—intelligent and gifted with imagination—sat behind his desk, with his pungent cigar-smell among heaped up papers of land-registry, notarised deeds, certificates yellow with age and duly signed contracts, patiently weaving a multicoloured web full of dreams.

But as Rivermaid always appeared to them glistening with pearls and scented with lemon balm, while they were always crowded together in huts, the people believed that, one day which would go down in history, they would catch a little share of beauty, if only a dusting of fine gold from her eyelids. And each one dreamt his own dream of the comb she used to smooth her hair, as long and beautiful as her woman's shape from another world. And so they dreamed until the day when the first fine layers of dust began to cover the plants, then the river water washed down the debris of a land feeling the first tremors of agony.

The little girl who had heard about Rivermaid in the stories didn't believe in her moon or in her comb, until, on that afternoon all sicklied over with a twilight sun, after singing over and over *Eel in de water* to catch a little clean water to wash her panty stained with the blood of her first period, she had seen just a few arm-lengths out in the river, the marvellous creature scented so sweetly with citronella and lemon balm.

And there was the comb shining on the rock.

The Wanderer, whose memory was the first thing to fail, had forgotten the luminous words she had whispered to the little girl, and how that evening she had gone to weep at the head of the girl's sleeping mat, waking with her moans the father, who shouted out in the darkness:

— Daughter, why you bawling? You hungry?

And he had armed himself with a machete the next night, because the girl told him it was not she who cried: she had dreamt mad things, like this unbelievably beautiful woman playing a sad tune on a guitar. Rivermaid did remember when the little girl with the comb had crossed the dried up river by the sandy path leading to the main road. In spite of everything she had followed the sad procession under the fierce Tropic of Cancer sun. Since that day, she never slept again. Her eyes were worn with weariness. She couldn't bear the weight of her heavy legs.

The Wanderer went back and forth in the room. The cracking of her skeleton sounded like a key turning in a rusty lock. She staggered among the papers covered with figures, the cigar-smell and Mister Longthread's sneezes exploding like an old rifle. He had caught cold during some heavy rains which must have been the time of the seven days' flood. He exploded at nose and mouth. The Wanderer, dragging herself painfully, threw her unlovely carcass at Mister Longthread's feet. That enormous personage shifted his office chair only in very exceptional circumstances. But since it was a question of reviving with blood and energy his sick and broken creature, he allowed his elephantine tail to slip down to the foot of his chair, and was shaken by a catastrophic motion which made his body quiver like a wet mammoth.

To perpetuate his power, Mister Longthread accepted the painful demands of this incestuous union. In the dark violence of their gestures, this couple, as stinking as the devil's wind, have for long centuries already been in intimate collusion amid the cigar smell, ashes, papers covered in figures, and the explosive sneezes crackling out in that well-appointed office like an old rifle being fired.

A silence fell over the ghetto. Unaccustomed and moonlike.

Since Walk-bout Woman's recent passing through, the oldest of her flock still throwing stones up at the clouds, a blue deathlike calm flowed down from the leafless tree on the heights of Death's-Door, slid through Seven-Dagger-Cut, hugged the corners of the shacks along I-believe-in-God alley before casting the giant shadow that spread over the whole vastness of the stars.

Raphael was coming home from a night-time story-telling, which now the old man less often held, still reciting the story of the beautiful brown girl and Diamond-Rivermaid's comb, of the massacre of dogs, the skinny madwoman and the plot of wild flowers where Bombardopolis woman was delivered of two puppies. In Raphael's memory the reprisals were still vividly alive, and he was anxious at this deep silence as he took the path to Passiona's little house with its whitewash which the years had faded, the sun dried out and now was tinted blue in the moonlight shining from higher up the slum. This outlying landscape bathed in a melancholy colour gave off faint smells of sea air, mixed with the sharp volcanic tang of the discoloured old plaster.

He met a drunken man addressing a wall as if entreating a ghost:

— O Mary Madeleine, me no go break down the door!

Come out with me and feel this moon! O Mary born without sin!

Raphael lengthened his strides.

The giant shadow of the silence. The corners of the huts. Closed doors. A gleam of candle. A carpenter's notice. A chair-leg on the road. A shop sign. A window opening. The heat. The sea smell. This agonised blue.

He recognised the passageways by their smells. But he'd never heard such silence since he'd been born in the shacks. Evenings are always the noisiest times, with gaming, dominoes, the foul-mouth chat of a whore, poor people coming and going, children shouting: life begins for them in the evening. He couldn't understand why everything was suddenly struck dumb. Why the ghetto was still as a grave. He hurried along.

The church bell struck a time he couldn't make out. The bell sound clapped over all the huts like a sinister night bird.

The giant shadow of the silence. The passageways. The moon. The heat. The silence. The silence.

— Beast!... sst!... sst!... sst!... sst!...

The echo of a voice cut through the evening like a knife.

Raphael thought it was the drunken man again, but when a laugh followed the voice with a mighty roar, he knew it was something more, and he ran off as fast as his legs would carry him.

— Ah!... Ah!... Ah!... Ah!...

The laugh was gaining power.

In spite of the jolly drunkards, in spite of the warm night atmosphere of the old brothel, with its Mexican saloon melodies going on till dawn, in spite of the Holy Water Saturday when *Vivi* had been paraded, in spite of the horse's neigh, in spite of the 'paniard girls squawking like Guinea-hens, there is this word of truth: rootless people don't laugh. The slum knows neither laughter nor tears, only sometimes a shout, as when they scream: We hungry! and the midday bell lets you hear the bawling of all the little sons of all the

Dinombiens at the gate of heaven. Even when the rose laurels were crowding the roofs, shading the narrow window openings, decorating the legs of old tables like humble altars, or winding into the lanes and the passageways like sunlit haloes, no one ever showed any joy like that at the Feast of Flowers. Besides it was forbidden to sing about little rose-bush full a stars.

That moonlit night in the world of the dispossessed, the laugh grew stronger; without any visible source, like the voice of an old ghost.

— Ah!... Ah!... Ah!... Ah!...

Raphael could feel the laughter in his head, behind the silent huts, deep in the passageways, on the old zinc roofs, on a doorstep. Panic-stricken, he'd lost his way in this maze of moonraked alleys, marked only by the howling dogs. He turned into dead ends, retraced his steps, struck into a side alley, took a right fork, dashed to the left, spun around.

— Ah!... Ah!... Ah!... Ah!...

It wasn't in a single throat any more. It was hundreds. The laugh took on giant proportions. It echoed back and forth through the ghetto, growing louder and louder. The world of the lost people erupted into such loud and sonorous laughter that the whole city woke up in the middle of the night, believing a hurricane was coming or an earthquake. First the lights went up in every window of the presidential palace like a great dove. Then the army barracks lit up. Then the houses. One by one. Then the villas. Then the gardens. Then the ornamental fountains. Then the hotels and their swimming pools. Then the guest houses. Then the church presbyteries. Then the cathedral. Then the bars. Then the shops. Then the pharmacies. The streets. The lanes. The avenues. The casino. The bakers. The dead ends. The pork butchers. The supermarkets. The whole city lit up.

And the world was bright as if the sun had suddenly risen over huge cities wallowing in their night-time sins. The enormous echo of the laughter went on growing and growing until the whole country was shaken as if by a seismic shock.

— Ah!... Ah!... Ah!... Ah!...

The tremor, the enormous laugh, terrified sailors and travellers on the Caribbean Sea, spread to other islands where it also began in the slums, all the dusting of islands like fallen stars studding this region of cane, bauxite, bananas and flames-of-the-forest. It followed the curve of the Alantic, was sucked into the Magellan Straits, turned up towards the Tropic of Capricorn and was blown away by the trade winds, down from the high blue peaks of Aconcagua, in a gigantic rumble of thunder—volcanic bursts of sound lasting for many hours, and eventually dying away at the north window in the early polar morn to the tune of *América Latina* which they were still dancing to in an old brothel scented with lazy dawns.

On that deep and mighty night, all the slums of the lands of the centre and the south erupted into a volcanic laugh discharging vast flows of debris, songs, moon fragments, as if liberating for a new universe. The laugh bore away masks, decorated floats, Carnival devils, whiskers from the moustache of a former general, old dresses of women long buried, banners washed out by the rains, paper flags faded by seasons when hails of bullets re-echoed, and all the things which were passing away, grating or whining, sad and majestic puppets who had set for ever in a hollow grin.

He hadn't got out of their moon. And only the howl of dogs had answered the shout John sent through Passiona's window. At least, that was what he'd heard in the dimly-lit little room full of the scent of mint: after his shout, just the howling of dogs. He'd never believed his son, who couldn't find words to convey that enormous laugh suddenly bursting out after the voice had spoken. It was this laugh that was the answer from all the dispossessed to that terrible word which John had flung in the direction of the yellow barracks. Though John admitted saying *beast*, he couldn't get used to the idea that his voice might have echoed over all the ghetto to the point of arousing such grand comedy. Longing in spite of everything to overcome this disbelief, Raphael kept on so about the voice and the laugh that one day, unable to contain his anger any longer, for the first time John raised his broad hand, all hardened with engine grease, to hit his son.

If Passiona hadn't intervened, he would have had a bone broken for sure. After this threatening, Raphael went for days without going to meet his father when he came home with his dusty old machine, not speaking to him, not even looking at him, so that he didn't notice the beard John was growing to force him to look up at his sorry self. He regretted his actions so much, that he was full of embarrassment about how to get close to his boy. And this went on until the morning when, as the dawn faded behind the hovels and the piss from chamber pots was emptied into the lane, Walk-bout Woman returned with her flock and her mysterious bundle. John saw his son dash off, like all the other boys, towards the old vagabond. Without stopping to think, with a breath of morning on his lips, he shouted to him:

— Where you going, Raphael?

— Catch me if you can! came the answer.

Suddenly happy, he sped off behind his son with such energy that he almost broke an ankle. And they arrived together, all out of breath in the middle of the little flock, bursting with laughter at the game.

That same morning John made the acquaintance of the worker Dorismé.

He'd come to learn the news carried on Walk-bout Woman's bundle, and heard with delight that, the night before, the lights had gone up all over the town because of an enormous laugh which seemed to come from the slums. But he noticed he wasn't the only one who was pleased: John and Raphael were laughing. Dorismé went up to them, believing that these strangers too could decode the messages of the bundle. John and Dorismé spoke together briefly after shaking hands, then retired behind an old board house by a mud puddle to talk of their lives and hopes.

The bus man told Dorismé about the calvary of the city avenues with his old wreck trundling along in the sun, groaning like a TB patient at a spot of rain. He told him about his little shack, built with his own hands on the lands now taken by the vast *Incorrperaytid*.

The worker told the bus man about his journey to town: two hundred kilometers on foot with the men driving their cattle to the slaughterhouses of the capital. He told him about his months in jail for having stabbed a man who called him "brothel bastard". He told him how he'd just stood around until the day he'd found work in the big sheds.

The bus man recalled the dreadful time of three years, two months, three weeks and four days of drought, when the dogs barked with their muzzles to the sun; then the seven nights and seven days of unceasing rain and flood. By the mud puddle, behind the old board house, they told each other so many things they didn't notice time passing.

— Plenty more to do, said Dorismé. All a we just bones to rot in Jesus-Grave? We not going to give up and dead slowly, leaning on a old stick, telling all we troubles at the cathedral door, or in the market to them saltfish seller. Must do more to fill the pickney empty belly and stop them turning we people out a door. Flame-tree bloom strong in the hills. The river run cool on the black sand. Nothing not here but dust and filth. Must keep heartful or just fold up and dead. Everything against we, even these flies. Nothing to lose, man...plenty to win!

The day was brightening. All the sounds of life rang out along the lane like a great creaking of cart wheels. Blindmen, beggars, cripples, widows, women doing penance went by in the throng. The dogs watched them pass or wormed their way among them, attracted by the strong smell. Heaven looked down as they dragged their sad tatters along; the mud walls of the huts slowly cracked with their unheard laments. Who knows where they were heading. Morning had summoned them.

The two men by the mud pool separated with a will to do more. One went off to the big sheds, the other to his broken-down bus.

From that day John understood why the old vagabond woman drew so many children when she came down the lane of the shantytown with her ragged little tribe, looking up toward the sun.

100

PART TWO

Vèvè for Petro

The *Petro* rituals of voodoo, distinguished by pig sacrifices, special drumming and refrains of "Vive la liberté", invoke spirits of rage and revolt.

The rumour had been going around for days, repeated from window to window like good news. But the lost people had learnt to be sceptical, since the big speechifying campaign by the men from the sheds to persuade people that *Incorrperaytid* wasn't a slaughterhouse, and since the arrival of the mechanical box with pictures of babies at the breast, which had brought a time of deep mourning and an incredible shower of comets. So the lost people showed no wild enthusiasm, for when they bumped into each other down a passageway or nodded between hot sips of grog, it was obvious from their dismissive tones that they attached more importance to the story of Carmelia. She was a pure-bred negro woman, black as a funeral dress, married a year to a little cobbler man just as black as she, and to his shame (how he called down thunderbolts from heaven to strike down the deceiver!) she gave birth to a little mulatto girl with wavy hair. This business made so much noise, and raised such chat and laughter, that everyone forgot the rumour that a brand new marvel was going to come to the shanties. One morning, a shout was heard, and people opened their windows to see what it was:

— The poles have come!... The poles!...

In a cloud of dust rising up from the bottom of the steep slope leading to the heart of the slum, a sound of axles keeping time with heavy breathing indicated where hand-carts with wobbly wheels were painfully bearing the electricity poles.

So the marvel arrived one dusty morning. Holes had been dug with picks and shovels at each crossroads and at every twentieth shack. Contrary to expectation, people weren't celebrating the great event. An old mosquito-hunter, nowadays rather too fond of drink, but for all that still with the mind of a pioneer, spent a long while looking at this odd activity and couldn't resist thinking: "This time they come to plant their light on our dunghill!"

A few days later, when they'd finished putting up the poles and pulling the cables through, one evening heavy as an anvil, light suddenly flooded out at the crossroads. And the bright light created such panic among the homeless ones that they could be seen hiding their faces and eyes, groping for their crutches or their rags, and scuttling away towards darker places. They were frightened of this light which assaulted them in their misery.

The cables came from town, went through the guardpost, looped over the shacks and entered the vast domain of the big sheds.

Then began a struggle between the uprooted and the light. First came the children, who thought the cables would catch some breeze for their kites. When the first child was found at the foot of a pole, burned like a lump of charcoal with the kite string in his hand, it was Holy Week, and the dispossessed swore before heaven and Jesus Christ that they would get the better of that devil living in the wires. Sometimes, mad with rage at these cables which refused to give up their diabolical secret and still kept flinging down charred bodies at their feet, the people stoned the lamps and broke them. One evening, at the time when the light was usually switched on around the *Incorrperaytid* compound and under the guardpost awning, it came only faintly, preventing the machines from working and enraging the man with the horse's neigh, who could not see the curve of his whore's breasts. A shout of victory came from the shanties, each lit up like a little lantern, transforming the ghetto into a magic vision. In the heat of the night, a mysterious wild chant went up, carrying into the distance as far as the slums on the edge of the city. But the next day the guards came, the man with the horse's neigh and his henchmen. They went into the shacks, broke the bulbs, cut the wires with pincers and beat anyone who protested. Thick night covered the slums again, pierced only by the lamps at the crossroads. Those majestic sentinels, the poles, held skeletons of kites prisoner in their tops. The dogs, who had been relatively quiet since the time of the reprisals began to bark again, pissing at the foot of the heavy poles, and pointing their muzzles in the direction of the midday breeze, which bore on its back the sound of the cathedral bells.

It was at that time, when death was again taking a heavy toll, that, after years of forgetting her, John met down a passageway a mint-scented woman who seemed to be waiting for him and who was an old, old friend. His drooping tail like a turkey's wattle, those turtles with young ladies' heads, the powdered cheeks of the fat madam, the white man who reeked of tobacco: for a few brief seconds all that past time flashed through his memory, before he touched Madeleine's hard icy fingers. She wore an angelic smile, and was dressed in white linen like a madonna. The breeze stirred the folds of her dress. The half-moon rode in the sky. Madeleine seemed to be floating through a magical plantation of stars. The scent of mint glided over the blueish ghetto night. To John she appeared so pure, so lovely, that he couldn't believe that he had held this moon maiden for nights on end clutched to his chest. They drifted along, as if caught up in a beautiful dream, under shopsigns smeared with soot, past doors eaten away by bad weather, beside windows jammed in their frames, brushing past a drunk, a dog, or a smell of mud, talking of the past in low voices, looking at the sickle-shaped moon, hearing the cries of children in the dark, until, a few steps away from an old café where they could just hear the languid tune of a *romancero*, John felt the cold hand he was holding turn hard as stone and the woman beside him collapse like a sudden landslide: all that was left of her in the moonlight was a heap of bones, with leg bones, slender finger bones and the sparkling clean enamel of white teeth sticking out. John stood like a statue.

Madeleine had died on the 4th May in the Year of the Flood.

The next day when John came back to the place, all he could see where the bones had been was a stinking mud puddle. Only the white sheets smelling of soap and the women's underwear hanging up on the flat roofs of the brothel, scented lingerie drying in the sun like doves, reminded him of the dazzling dress of the ghost who had wanted to return to tell her man she hadn't survived the itching of a cancerous womb.

It was the month of flowers and they had given her a fine funeral. When the people in the old café had heard the news of her death in the hospital, they had stopped drinking and laughing. The old madam had taken up a collection and raised three hundred and fifteen dollars. Two days after, on the 6th May, on that luminous warm afternoon when the funeral procession got under way down the main slum track, there were so many flowers, wreaths, white dresses, ladies' picture hats, handkerchiefs and veils, that the crowd of bystanders gave their view with a touch of irony.

— This whore funeral more like a parade to honour the Holy Virgin!

The scent of Madeleine's funeral lingered for days along the lane. It needed the action of sun, moon, dust and breeze to dispel what remained. The only time people remembered anything similar was the day in the season of Golgotha hues when there passed nearby—on the anniversary of a Revolution full of betrayals and faded slogans—the heavy black limousines of the Presidential cortege, with their twilight brocade interiors. Like the tails of meteors they sped along, enveloped in a shower of coins and new bank-notes bearing the likeness of the Mighty Father, among little paper flags in the national colours, under picturesque triumphal arches of rose laurel, amid the hysterics of the light-skinned women at the windows of their balconies, amid the cheering and the puddles, amid the multicoloured patchwork of good-luck blouses, amid the whole world of rottenness. The cortege went by, as shooting stars go by, trailing a wake of mermaid's hair, followed by a crowd the colour of a sandal's sole, clashing jaws, jostling, head down like rams, to catch on the wing the bank-notes thrown from the car windows like birds. It passed between the shacks, the cathedral bells ringing for the *Te Deum* and the fanfare of trumpets of the angels of the Ascension; the cortege went by with such a cosmogony of gunfire, brilliant decorations and old medals that it seemed to be heading for the sky the colour of the beginning of the world. The President! Lord, but we must go tell him that! That me little sister hungry, that moma can't find a cent, and that papa, poor soul, him dead Thursday and they throw him down a hole. Must tell 'im! The electricity, must tell 'im thanks, and the corn they give out the other day. Long live the President! The little boy threw himself into the crowd, trampled on, pushed around, shoved about by the others, must tell 'im! Must tell 'im everything! He couldn't hold on to anything, and felt himself being lifted off the ground. That moma spend months looking work in the *Incorrperaytid*, and every time she come home tired, 'cause she spend every day looking at lock gate. Must tell 'im! He felt himself falling with all his weight. He tumbled into the thick dust of the road and, covered with mud and fine dust, saw the gloomy meteors fly off among the flowers and rottenness towards the sky the colour of the beginning of the world.

The young boy went back down the dusty road, with the bling-binding of the festival in his head, and in the hollow of his belly something like a sad dance of death. He could smell the bitter burnt-out-planet smell of these meteorites that sped along amid the cheering and the puddles, making the depths of the passageways stink so violently with an ill-defined dead animal smell that when Dormelia rubbed her indigo ball in the tinted water of her white enamel bowl, she was suddenly assaulted by this gust of rotten shit in the middle of her sad washerwoman's song. She stood up in a panic, as if the devil was after her, and searched feverishly in the little room of planks and cardboard without managing to find the source of the smell. She went out of the door the width of a coffin which gives on to the yard of pig mud, nostrils flaring in the wind, following the track of the smell.

She passed among long sad dirty children, stepped over an old car body where a hen was sitting on her eggs, bucked with her left foot against a can of Shell Company gasoline, met some boys blowing soap bubbles in the air beside an outhouse with a door the Virgin's blue, and stopped, suffocating and astonished, in front of a wet pair of trousers hanging on a line. Besieged by the flies and sniffed by a dog, the trousers seemed to be crucified on that wire in their overpowering smell of rotten shit. Not since the time when she'd been imprisoned in the yellow barracks with the flag on top had she ever smelt such a smell, not even when she untied the knot of the huge bundle of dirty linen which she had to wash and press for the Day: pants, merinos with holes, shirts, underpants and socks all together had never reached such an extreme. And yet she had almost rubbed her hand raw scrubbing those uniforms the colour of a stormy sea in the long week leading up to the anniversary of the Revolution—uniforms from the army barracks, the national penitentiary, the yellow guardposts. But the man with the horse's neigh nearly killed her twice over, because there was no way, without risking court martial, that he could celebrate that illustrious day with a pair of trousers that smelled of rotten shit. Yet the nearer drew the day, the less the smell would go away. Exhausted, Dormelia had strung them up on the wire in the hope that the night dew and the noonday sun could do better. Not a chance. So that was the reason why the man with the horse's neigh was not to be seen under the rough triumphal arch he'd had made out of coconut and rose laurel boughs, and under which the procession did not pass. Trembling with fear, red with rage, hiding his civilian trousers behind the barrack window, he was wild enough to cut off his own finger when one of his men came up and told him that the building of the arch had all been for nothing: instead of the presidential cortege, gangs of criminals had passed, who tore it to bits. A few hours after the procession had gone by, he loaded his revolver, and with three of his men got into an old carnival-coloured Buick which set off like a bomb over the wreckage of the arch, the dust and dead flowers. They'd gone to hunt for Dormelia.

— Jesus Mary Joseph! Revolution Day today!...

At once she gauged the danger threatening her in view of the dripping trousers. Hastily she made up a little packet, and left wide open the door of the little room where there was nothing but a chair and a mat. Dormelia hurried off down the twilit passageways, anguish in her eyes.

Night had not yet begun to fall when the dispossessed, still recalling the distant time of the terrible stench of plague, sent smoke billowing through all the slum to dispel the odour of that turbulent day. When the moon came up behind the dark roofs, the night was scented with nutmeg from the blueish rays falling on this old land of marshes, shacks and manhunts in the gloom. Dormelia's squat and breathless shadow crossed the nameless alleys that disappear into the maw of night. She sped through brief gleams of lamplight, through the mournful rattle of the wind deep in the passageways, with the dismal cry of an owl overhead. She sped like a silent star.

Stale dawn and faded camelia adorned her, as in the pale light and tired as a donkey, she stepped between the puddles of still water and the first piss pots poured down the lane of the Flower-Town quarter, where you could still see the old termite-eaten wood of the latrines, the faded signs nailed up over the shop-doors selling oil, saltfish and stale biscuits, the stumps of rose laurels which had seen so many doves taken flight, so many moons wax and wane, so many children die, the discoloured whitewash of the cottages beaten by the dust and the rain....

So many things which brought to mind those heroic days when the mosquito-hunters, smelling of smoke and mud, built their huts of strong clay between the marshes and the stars, and marked out the passageways by giving them the name of the first event that occurred there. One such concerned this poor woman who, when she least expected, felt her back bones creaking terribly and was delivered of a poor little seven-month babe, so blinded by moonshine and quailed by the cold breeze whistling down the lane, that he cried out twice, too loudly for his age, and died right then, all sticky in his mother's arms. She'd remembered those cries all her life, every time she took the alley named Seven-month-a-bawl. Dormelia went down this same alley with its sooty doors, gasps of exhaustion and pain escaping from her toothless mouth, and then an endless litany of Jesus-Mary-Joseph save your servant after three gunshots rang out in the distance, in the silence of the dawn. These killed the poor bread seller, too simple to know his name or his trade: his only crime was waking early, as he did every Monday before the Pole Star set, to go and fetch hot bread from Rosaire's bakery. The lost people hadn't woken out of their sick animal sleep, accustomed as they were to the insane caprices of the man in the yellow barracks: getting up at cock-crow, about every three days he used to go and fire shots down the black hole of his own latrine, whose smells were all of his own making, since he forbade the use of it even to his henchmen. During the night she had tried to get out of the slum, but they were keeping watch at all the exits, and Dormelia had to resort to forgotten paths, though she had known them in her childhood, winding beside the plague-ridden mosquito creeks and along which arrived caravans of folk carrying their bundles of troubles, their cooking pots, their kids, their rags and their thirst, like sad camels crossing a desert.

It was by these miry tracks that one afternoon as yellow as fever she had seen coming an old crone, dirty as a dug-up coffin, who dangled a bundle clattering with saucepans. It was the day the Old Hag had come.

From the time of that vision in the afternoon, she had bad dreams she could never interpret, until one in which she saw a soldier with polished shoes and medals sparkling like little mirrors who marched up and down in her tiny room. She didn't know how, but the next day she got work in the barracks. It was along these same leprous paths that people said they'd seen coming the beautiful brown girl who'd stolen the Rivermaid's comb. Dormelia had only seen her the day before the flood began, on the dusty road leading to the fountain. The washerwoman wasn't thinking about these things when she knocked on Passiona's door, and John came out, saying to her solemnly, as he held out a beaker of cool water:

— We going save you from that dutty beast.

And it was Raphael who guided them through the rocky gullies where wild flowers grew and under old wooden bridges which had been thrown across the ravines scoured out by the overflow from the drain. At last they reached the top of a mound in a kind of old structure made of volcanic rock, now ruined and hidden among the thickets. It was all that was left of Fort Mercredi: one of those built by intrepid heroes to keep watch over a too blue sea which still smelled of the Conquistadors' bitter foam, whose ghostly galleons brought gunpowder, shackles and the pox. In a lair dug into the rock they found Wet-Back waiting.

A few years later, facing the firing squad among ten or so men standing at the edge of Jesus-Grave, in the last dawn of a July morning, Dormelia would remember this man who received her like his child and talked to her about a freedom that she never knew, accustomed as she was to her dunghill life. Like a beast of burden, her chest was sunk in and her breasts, which had never given suck, hung down dry.

But there was once a time of great terror, when by St. Joseph's Gate, peasants from the north armed with machetes and knives descended upon the city and set up camp in the courtyard of the National Palace. They washed in the blue water of the ornamental ponds, tore down the rose laurels in the Pantheon Square and bellowed like cows released into a pasture. Then Dormelia was only three months grown in the belly of a woman, who, weary of breeding children four at a time, had crossed the deserted main street of the city to plant herself in front of the rebel *cacos* who were breaking down the door of a store selling cloth, clocks and soap:

— Kill off this litter for me, she'd shouted at their knives, lifting her loose pink *moumou* right up to her chin. Instead they had blessed her, flashing the bloody blades of their raised machetes:

— Is we woman a bear the flame of revolution!

Her brave mother, who had bared her body to the *caco*

bands and had seen the death of an old general called Thélémaque perched on his rocking chair, didn't have time to tell her daughter the story because she passed away a few months after giving birth to her frail little girl.

The flag on the end of a gnarled tree branch which flew from the top of the yellow barracks had already faded from bad weather; and try as they would with jail, beatings, demolishing shacks and daily violence, the guards there couldn't think what to do to track down the washerwoman. The only thing that put a stop to this death hunt was the apocalyptic news circulating throughout the country: the coming of the end of the world.

Almost half a century had passed since the first announcement had come, with all its lists of special dates, predictive calculations and zodiac cycles, together with sermons full of funereal trappings, open tombs, walking dead with their ammoniac smell and the blaring trumpets of Jericho. In these days this whole great region of shacks was only an uncertain landscape of swamps, locked in the indifference of the moons and the seasons. The sun set in a great twilight behind the marshes, in the pungent air of the salt flats, with a strange silence only broken by the siren of a cargo boat seeking its mooring at the old city wharf.

Although they had lived through many false prophecies, people were still dazzled by this promise of all the old dreams in the world. This time the news took on such urgency that a week before the date predicted, the man-with-the-horse's-neigh caused the door of the barrack prison to be opened. And out came beings with a glassy stare, blinded by the sunlight. They disappeared into the passageways of the ghetto like sinister mummies. Seeing them pass like risen dead, a collective hysteria quickly spread. From door to door the news was repeated: Holy Virgin Mary! that Mésidor Dieusibon, dead this three years gone, been seen again that very day drinking water from a tin cup and leaning against a shack in Seven-month-a-bawl alley. The news that Malé Dorilas, dead from gangrene these four years, had been seen again that very day by a group of washerwomen, over by where the big shed wall started, looking for something which must be the place where his carpenter's bench used to be. The news that Brer Perceval, the old man who used to tell stories about the beautiful brown girl who stole the Rivermaid's comb—he'd mysteriously disappeared at the time of the reprisals—had reappeared that day, calling out just as he used to do to the children who didn't answer his call. So many visions of resurrection that the whole district lived through a week of fantasies.

When the great day at last arrived, from the first light of dawn, processions of women with flowers had gone to the big Cathedral Square. Then by every path and track dense groups thronged in, feeling the spirit, their heads raised towards heaven. Chanting rose up on every hand: vibrant hosannas, alleluias. But the great door of the cathedral had remained shut, and no priest dared to appear before a crowd waiting more fervently than ever for the gift of eternal life. The slums emptied of their poor, their sick, their miserly shopkeepers who hadn't thought it safe to leave their money behind and carried it with them knotted into grubby handkerchiefs. Paralytics who couldn't walk had themselves carried. And they all came down the lanes smelling of rose laurel, arms open wide to the blue, blue sky. In the ghettos the breeze blew in the depths of the passageways. They had the look of regions deserted in a great plague. Voices in the big crowd could scarcely be heard, but from the top of the mound of old Fort Mercredi you could see, in the window of a hut perched on the slopes of the hill, one lone individual, an old artist. In a strong smell of turpentine and linseed oil, he was painting a canvas propped up on a chair which depicted a vast paradise, a painting commissioned from him by an art-dealer in town. As if deaf to the echoing hosannas, the old painter, with a cigarette butt at the corner of his lips, went over the vivid green and blue on his canvas; and slowly, squeezed into that small room, the vast paradise took shape, the collective dream of all those thousands in the Cathedral Square. Soon it would be packaged and freighted to the north, stamped *Made in West Indies*.

— This Resurrection is nothing but boss man whore. But real Resurrection-time when man and woman stand up tall, they can't touch that, you hear me!

This was Dorismé speaking, having come at dusk to the old fort while the disillusioned throng went back to their shacks. He'd met Dormelia, who had been with all the others singing and waiting for eternal life.

— But what bout all these dead people going around from Saint Martin to Grande Saline? I see with me own eyes Aristide Boutenégre, that old drunk man from by Jesus-Grave, beat his wife out a door and she still in mourning for him. Him say she not pleased to have him back, but she fraid fe him duppy eye, and him arm so thin and full of ticks, like he just dug up from the grave!...

She stumbled over an old cannon lying in the tall grass which had grown up among the ruins. The breeze carried across to the crest of the hill the sharp tang of the sea, mingling with the smell of the alleyways winding through the squalid space below. High above the panorama of roofs, Dormelia looked where Dorismé was pointing; the old flag faded by many storms was flapping gloomily over the yellow barracks, stirred by the warm wind coming off the sea. "See it there our dutty grave, our pit!" he'd said to Dormelia, up among the daisies growing in the glades, the cannon in their eternal sleep, and the first stars, so close that you'd think you could hold them just by stretching out a hand. And Dormelia recalled a story, how five prisoners had mysteriously escaped on the eve of their execution: one with faith had drawn a little sailing ship on the wall of the cell, and they all sailed away on it like ghosts. But she knew very well the only way you got out of that place was to be eaten alive by all the vermin of the land and the sea-floor. She no longer believed in this judgement day, but no one could convince her that they weren't resurrected dead who were walking around down there with their smell of corpses in formalin and their faces like the far end of the apocalypse. At least until the morning when she met the old storyteller Brer Perceval dragging himself along with his stick and reciting at every door and under every window that the beautiful brown girl, who had travelled the roads and slept under the stars with Rivermaid's comb, had left this old place of swamps, won over by the tears of an officer, who at the time of the reprisals had been felled like an ox by the most beautiful eyes in the world. Some said the old man had turned quite foolish. But those who had seen on very hot nights a car with no number-plates going down the main slum track and a man getting out who disappeared into the maze of smaller passages, sometimes with a flash of moon on his shoulder, those people paid more heed, and spread the news that the brown girl who made the rose laurels grow had been stolen away. And in truth, since the news got about, the flowers had stopped growing, and those that had climbed over the old roofs of the huts withered one by one.

A second time of drought was about to begin. It was heralded one midday by the howling of dogs all over the slum. Then there was a terrible heat beating down from the sky. One morning a woman opened her window, and with a great wail displayed the body of her child, whose tongue was hanging out right down the chin. Then people recognized the terrible signs and knew that they were going to relive the doom-stricken days of sun, dust and thirst. This time there was also an epidemic of plague, followed by the fast-spreading blue fever. Candles in the churches at the feet of St. Roch and his son, flowers in the tabernacle of St.

Charles Borromeo, couldn't check the scourges. The sick crawled off to inoculate the city with their misery. For quenching his thirst in the gutter, a beggar was beaten to death. The city grew frightened.

The police drove the beggars and ragged ones back into their flea-ridden reserves, and barriers were built to shield the city centre from the shantytowns of the uprooted, who carried in their blood, in the air they breathed, on their skin, Death's own virus.

For the sixth time the colonel had silently pushed open the door to gaze in the soft light of the bedside lamp and between the diaphanous moons, flowers and butterflies of the mosquito net upon the oriental grace of the woman's body, reclining on silken cushions and the embroidered sheet, like a dream fragment fallen onto a royal couch.

The first time was to take off her shoes. In spite of everything, she hadn't lost the habit of sleeping in her shoes. He had carefully removed them and bent over to inhale that faint wild animal smell given off by her delicate little feet newly bathed in eau de cologne with the toe-nails painted with a brick-red dye. Then he'd gone out, and after a time returned to take out the thumb which she kept in her mouth when asleep. The doctor who had come the week before had diagnosed a fixation at the oral stage and prescribed a medicine. The third time he came back with the pills and a glass of water, which he placed on the little cane table by the bed. The other times he didn't know what to do.

He could be seen going into the room, which smelt of rose laurel, looking vaguely at all the objects decorating the interior of his conquered territory: majestic powder-bowls in rosy glass, superb bottles of perfume in ornamental shapes, a chamber-pot resembling a real vase of flowers, a looking-glass as shiny as a lake in the moonlight, a gleaming mahogany wardrobe, a sewing machine with its needle still in a piece of sewing scarcely started, little bobbins of thread of every colour set out on an apron: all things she didn't want and which made her sullen in spite of the colonel's deep affection, until the day when into the midst of this fabulous decor came the simplest thing in the world, that for the first time filled her with joy: a little wicker chair.

She'd put it by her bed, and the colonel always found her sitting there, stitching away at a dress which never got finished.

The last time he'd pushed open the bedroom door, it was dawn. Light filtered through the glass window, and it was impossible to be sure which of the two, the colonel or the girl, was living the dream of a woman lying on the calm waters of a lake like a boat, a woman's body floating slowly upstream to a sound of drinking vessels and dishes as if in a phantom banquet, with something indistinct in her hair resembling a large blue clip. In her sleep, the beautiful brown girl was so obsessed by the brightness of the clip that she woke up in a fright and searched frantically for the comb which was under the pillow.

As when she lived in the slum, the brown girl never left her room, except to drag her steps through the silent house, whose washed mosaic floor reflected her shape of a proud camelia. Hours at a time would find her among the multicoloured bobbins of thread, turning the wheel of the sewing machine and sitting on the little chair. Sometimes this went on until quite late in the night, when the colonel for some reason or other hadn't come home. It was on one such night that her sleep-walking first began to reveal itself. With her arms hanging loose and a moonstruck expression she was seen going through doors which seemed to open by themselves, lingering in the courtyard by the pool of moon water, draping the airy brightness of her dress over the plants or becoming a flower herself among the laurels and roses.

One night when, weary of her crochet, she'd fallen asleep on the little chair, three hours later she had risen up in the same blaze of inspiration and left the silent house. The handful of people who'd seen her pass spoke of an uncanny shape crossing the Plague-Wall (as they called it) on the electric cable and passing over the hut roots, on that night filled wth groans between death, piss and stars. She followed the line of the wires as far as the big sheds. They reported that she shone like an April moon. That the dogs at the sight of her radiance curled their tails down under their bellies. At the time no-one could have the slightest faith in this strange apparition until the day of revelation when the vision re-appeared to all those massed in the cathedral square. In the intervening time of drought, the colonel, who watched every movement of his beautiful mistress, from her strange attachment to the little chair to her amazement the first time she saw the water work its wonders in the flush-toilet, the colonel knew nothing of the trances which drew her always towards the sad squalid huts. Long evenings he would spend with her turning over the pages of a heavy photograph album, in which alongside the plates of nameless members of a family were photographs of sabres, epaulettes, medallions, boots, gold braid, insignia, parades on the garrison square, and award ceremonies at the foot of the external staircase of the presidential palace with its pergola decorated in the national colours.

Yet she still remembered, in her lonely hours, the donkey crossing the dried-up river, where the woman appeared beseeching her with the sadness of a leafless tree. She also remembered the Virgin-Mary-ascending-into-heaven which her poor mother carried in her bundle through the streets of the town, looking for some disused plot to plant a hut. So many memories bound her to that poor place behind the Plague-Wall.

All it had was a long bench for the patients and a table where a man sat giving out name-by-name small bits of card. Yet this clinic (recently set up) drew each day a throng of poor people who needed the pretence of a medical permit to be allowed into town.

The days had lost their names, all covered in dust and sores. And then one sad Tuesday, the day of Ogun, among the flies, the heat, the sick, in the shifting roundness of women's breasts and sunbaked bodies giving off a dead animal smell, there came the man-with-the-horse's neigh in his fat carnival-coloured Buick. He was angry, for the night before one of his men had been found in a mud pool by the cemetery, his sex cut off with knives. Before he had finished his harangue, his men had started their work. And the people, in the confusion of flight, screamed, cursed and even flung rocks at the so-called clinic in the rage of despair.

The crowd of rootless ones scattered leaving behind the debris of conflict and swirls of dust, one with the crutch of a fallen comrade transformed into a weapon, another tearing the latch off a door or the leg off a kitchen table, some running from one passageway to another howling like hunted beasts, one with a shoemaker's knife, another shouting for armed resistance against the great epidemic of repression.

From door to door he ran, just as he used to dodge at night around the living quarters of the big sugar plantation across the border. Wet-Back had left his hiding place to rouse the slums against those barring the way out of the Plague-Wall. With lightning speed the whole ghetto soon knew his story: hunted for years because he defended the oppressed, he defied death in the land of the 'panish girls, succeeded in crossing the border, knew poverty, shame, hunger and thirst and wanted the people to say with him—Can't tek no more! A shout went up over by Death's-Door, another from the Flower-Town district, and all of a sudden there was big trouble coming.

They came with odd weapons and cries. They came with their rages and their filth; violent roots at the ends of their arms, the memory of poverty. They made their way towards the Plague-Wall. In spite of sporadic shots to halt them, they passed through the barrier and on towards the guardpost with a fearful sound of rusty iron, shouting voices and barking dogs. Heavy gunfire rang out from the yellow barracks with its faded flag on top. Amid the answering bang of guns from the old war, shrill whistling of bullets and the rumbling of rocks thrown as if from a grotesque catapult, Wet-Back, in a splendour of dust and heroics, gave a shout which was taken up by other throats:

— People time now! Freedom now! Down with poverty!

Just then Dormelia, doing her laundry about three kilometers away in the stream, felt a call sounding in her left ear. She collected the linen blued with indigo and marched briskly towards the shanties. The guns barked out in the lowering daylight which stank of corpses and gunpowder. As Dormelia, all out of breath, appeared from a passage which opened onto the firing range soaked with the blood of the dispossessed, she saw Raphael with a kitchen knife in his fist, crossing the lane which separated the men of the yellow barracks from the rebels waiting in ambush behind

behind the bullet-riddled huts.

— Jesus Mary Joseph and all the saints in Heaven! Raphael!

Her voice drew the attention of the others. Wet-Back recognized John's son and leapt into the open under the wild hail of bullets. In his frantic dash, he was hit in the shoulder. Clutching his bleeding wound, he saw Raphael press forward again with his kitchen knife.

— Don't kill 'im, you set a pigs! he shouted in the direction of the barracks. A second bullet smashed into his chest. The man of Pedernales fell to his knees. For a few brief seconds, he saw again María Isabel, her unquiet spirit condemned to eternal wandering. He saw again his old comrades, he saw again the *capataz* felled by the machete blow.

— Band a coward, I would a cut off you balls! He dragged himself forward, bleeding and beautiful, arms raised and still shouting:

— Now they coming: People time a come!

A third bullet pierced his neck. Wet-Back fell face down, full in the midday sun, under the thunderous sound of hundreds of feet which trampled his body, making for the yellow barracks. Gone mad, the people destroyed it with rockstones and rage. It was as if they had demolished the place with blows from their bare heads, knees and fists.

Sitting in the carnival-coloured Buick, the man-with-the-horse's-neigh and his deputy Bramoulé Kandjolus tried to flee the fury of the uprooted. Before they had time to start the motor, the confused mass fell upon the front of the car like vultures, crushing the hood and doors. A few minutes later, all that remained was a flattened object in the dust. It lay in the middle of the main track with the strangeness of a dug-up prehistoric carcass, as if from a lost era. As if from the bowels of that swampy land fertilised with the blood of its pioneers had been extracted this smoking monster, formed in the burning sun of a Tuesday of suffering and rebellion.

It was now some hours since the big black butterfly had settled on the windscreen with the painted cracks that looked like a golden sun bursting out on the glass. John had chased it away. It came back again. "Bad news for me", he thought. Before he'd had time to think further, he saw on the sidewalk Dormelia all bedraggled and signalling to him to stop.

When they reached the old fort, where Dormelia had carried Raphael who'd been hit by a bullet, they could see an impressive military force armed to the teeth, surrounding the whole shantytown where the revolt had broken out. The crowd—all control lost—was moving towards town as if instinctively aware that its arrogant wealth, luxury stores, neon lights, long avenues, even its brothels, were their silent torturers. But the lost people were driven back with gun-butts into their reserve. There were no tears in Dormelia's eyes. But in the wrinkles of her aged face you could feel that suffering was reaching its limits. She said not a word.

— Papa! Raphael struggled to say.

— Me son! me son! You never should a!...Should a hide yourself!

— Is you tell me "when you a man, must have brave heart, not live like coward"....

— But..., a tear came to his eye,—but you not a man yet.

I tell you....

— I am a big man now. I know that neighbour Heloferne want bread for him woman and him pickney who no have none. I see him, poor man, in the middle of the lane with blood in 'im mouth. I remember Dinombien who did have blood in him mouth same way. I don't want to see you too papa with blood in you mouth. So I go ketch up you old kitchen knife. I did think it was my duty as your son...

— The guard them block off the place, said Dormelia, Jesus Mary Joseph!...

— Papa, why they block up we homes with the big board fence?

John felt his body collapsing with the weight of his sorrow. For he was living the final moments of his son's life. He gathered all his strength to answer with his eyes veiled in tears:

— Is because them don't like we smell. Ram-goat and shit is what we smell of. They mek us do it in front of we own house door so we understand we is just a piece of nastiness!...

He clenched his fist on his knee so hard you could hear the bones crack.

— You don't teach me yet, Papa, to drive the old Ford.

— She meking too much noise, seem like the rod them dropping off. You would feel 'fraid. She won't drive straight.

Passiona and Dorismé arrived at the first signs of dusk, completely shattered. Only when he came out of the big sheds had Dorismé heard the news and gone to warn Passiona, who was still at her trinket stall.

— They kill him, John! Comrade Wet-back dead!

— They take me son too!

Passiona fell upon Raphael, sobbing.

— Mama, he said in a voice that had no strength left. Me love you. Must finish with these people that say we smell of ram-goat and shit... Papa, tell me you going be brave...

— Raphael!...

— Tell me, papa. That one day you going to have a pretty white house. That one day me will have a little brother that won't know me at all, but every day he will be happy with bread to eat and toy to play with and mama to love him. Promise me now. Life can't be all stinking ram-goat and shit!...

— I promise, I promise you, me son....

— Papa!... his voice was growing weak.

He opened his eyes and breathed his last, with a look that was bright as a star.

John spent the whole night weeping beside the body. He couldn't bear it. His reason for living was there. When the first light of morning swept into the refuge in the old fort, his face was so ravaged with grief and reduced so suddenly to skin and bone that the new expression of harshness and power coming from him was almost unrecognisable. Passiona and old Dormelia came back with water, leaves, powder and perfume to lay Raphael out. They perfumed him with sweet basil water, sage bush and lotions, then laid him out on a bed of banana leaves. Surrounded by bouquets of white and pink rose laurel, Raphael had recovered as if by magic the purity of his features, the fullness of his lips and at moments John could believe that he was only resting.

It was in one of these fleeting moments that John seemed to see his boy rise slowly from his bed of banana leaves, climb the little time-worn stair and search frantically for something in the long grass of the courtyard of the old fort. Then he came back sadly, climbed down the little stair and stretched out again. John who, the first evening of this vision, believed he could hear some plaintive sobs which must be coming from his son, searched his memory for what it could be that was so important to Raphael. He thought of the pigeons. But at that time it was impossible to find any in the ghetto. Big migrations of doves always preceded

127

the bad times: reprisals, drought, floods, famine, as if to warn the race who were no longer nomads. He thought of the old kitchen knife. Dormelia had given it to him. John had thrown it in the grass, still stained with the blood of the man Raphael had cut before he was hit by the bullet. The last time the boy must have seen it was on the afternoon of the third day he lay sick.

John remembered that the boy had bent down to pick up the knife and had gone forward toward the old cannon.

He had scraped it with the blade, as if he wanted to remove the rust of the Season of Neglect, as if to tell his father to keep his promise. That those brave ancestors who forged this free nation, floating like a bird on the blue of the Caribbean Sea, should not be forgotten.

John would remember the sound of that blade on the old cannon in the ruined fort.

When he got the two thousand gourdes for *Our Lady of August* to pay for Raphael's funeral, John recalled the man who'd sold him the old crate in order to go to Nassau.

It was in a fine drizzle of rain that the sad procession of ten or so people got under way. Dorismé and John were at the head of the coffin, wet through. Old Dormelia leant on Passiona and their steps grew heavier with the mud on the road. The two poor women mingled their tears with the drops of rain. Also in the procession were two workmates of Dorismé. In the rear, with her eternal bundle, came Walkbout Woman with the last child left to her, the boy who threw stones at the moon. They arrived at the little cemetery where wild flowers had sprung up between the flat dilapidated tombs. Dorismé dug the grave in the cool muddy ground. John was planted straight as a tree beside the coffin set down by the clods of earth. When they slipped the bier into the grave and threw earth on to it, and he could no longer see the coffin which had been held up till then between the rain and the mud, John raised his fist and shouted into the sad afternoon.

— Me son Raphael Johnny Dove not dead, oonu murderers!

Heavy, huge, with its cranks, toothed wheels, gears and steady breathing: the Machine didn't belong to John. *Our Lady of August*, she had been his. Three thousand gourdes down, bathed with mint, her bodywork repainted, placed under the protection of his patron saint: she had measured up to the scope of his dreams. Of course the old crate had smelt bad and creaked her bones when she wasn't oiled.

— And yet she have a name from heaven, a fine name, I couldn't find better. I did have this dream I can never forget, where I stand in front of the tabernacle of Our Lady of the Rosary, with flowers in me hand. I know I must tek the name of this woman with her bare neck, no jewel, no chain, no gold band upon her. But her foot them beautiful for true. When I put me lip down, her foot them icy and hard, it seem her whole body did tremble with the poor sufferer kiss.

But this one, the Machine he worked on since his son's death, had no name. It was just called the Machine.

— One day when I have enough, I feel to give it a name. And the desire to bring it closer to his arms and hands grew so strong that one morning a fellow-worker helped him write *Passiona* in large letters on the Machine.

That was the day he was called in with some commotion to the office of the manager of *Incorrperaytid* to be told,

130

''The Machine doesn't belong to you, for Chrissake!'' It was the property of Mister Longthread. There were a lot of them in the high windowless sheds that retained a terrible heat. The sweat of the workers, the rumbling of the machines, the noise of the wheels: it had taken a long time to get used to this infernal rhythm.

Now, as John went into the office, the manager didn't look up from reading his paper; but John felt such a coolness, never in his life had he experienced such a purified, soundless atmosphere. John thought he understood that day where the man found the right to treat him and his comrades like stupid animals:

— Him live in paradise, while we dying in hell.

The walls of the big sheds were continually encroaching on the ghetto. John had to admit that the death of the man-with-the-horse's-neigh and Bramoulé Kandjolus hadn't halted the advance of the gigantic walls which towered over the shacks and drove men and skinny cattle towards the marshes and the flies, where the smell of the salt flats merged with the rough breath of the sea. The breeze carried that smell of old dunghill, of corpses drowned in the drain, of Dinombien, of Wet-Back, of his son, and left it on doors, walls, the linen hung on lines, in the air of the Flower-Town quarter, as far as the helterskelter shacks of Death's-Door. On the hilltop, none of those grassy places were left where John, that distant day, had looked for the blue wisteria to cure Raphael's measles.

— He was all I did have to give me courage, you understand, me friend. The time I keep watch beside his body, I feel so low. I come near to kill meself. It did haunt me mind. That time Dorismé hold me up. Me boy dead with the kitchen knife in him hand to fight those bastard!

— I knew Dinombien, me friend. He lose a son like you, enough to go off him head. He work on that machine. Him was one of the first they take on, but he couldn't even give his boy a proper funeral. Then Dinombien get shot and we leave the corpse with a message to bring bad luck to the papas of this place. Next thing they take some of we comrade away. We don't know if they dead but we sure they hurt bad. Must fight back. Them use we like beast for labour and then thirsty for we blood.

It was several weeks later, on a day which dawned oppressively, that those few people opening their windows or emptying their pisspots into the gutter saw coming down the main track a wretched, handcuffed troop, shoved along by armed soldiers in the direction of Jesus-Grave. Within seconds the whole place was aroused to watch this sinister procession which was trailed by an empty cane cart. Some faces were recognized among the prisoners. The *Incorrperaytid* workers could make out, despite his emaciated features and beard, the trade union leader who first spoke up on their behalf, a few days before the death of the shed watchman. Other men taken prisoner since the big riot, who had held out in silence under torture, were also going to be executed by the firing squad.

Dormelia, who had friends among the prisoners, could not restrain herself, although John tried to pull her back. She thrust herself into the middle of the lane and drew herself up before the commanding officer:

— A monster born out a bitch's running belly, that's what you are! One day you going pay for this, you can't destroy the race!

She was quickly subdued by a soldier and shoved in among the condemned. Then she understood that she was going to suffer the same fate. She cursed them louder than before:

— You hands stink with blood!

The procession wound heavily onward. with the cart dragging behind.

— Cursing no use against them, said the trade unionist, who'd moved close to Dormelia. We lost plenty men, plenty blood. This parade just a trap to catch more. You know

Dorismé?... He lucky enough to be alive. I give me life for the cause. But just now when I go by the big shed, them have more land still. In prison I hear about the riot and Wet-Back dead...Is who you mourning for?—For John's boy. Him get hit by a bullet.—John, who is that?—A good man. A brother. The trade unionist studied her face.—Woman, you old!—I tell meself I shouldn't dead on me sleeping mat, but on the street, fighting for freedom.—Mother, you make us brave.

That morning at Jesus-Grave they executed the ten or so as an example. Dormelia refused to confess herself to the priest, and when the man in the cassock came over to him to administer the last rites, the trade unionist shouted out:— If you go up to heaven, Father, tell the good Lord we had enough of waiting for His paradise. He can burn it all down with His hellfire!

They piled the bodies in the cart, which trundled slowly down the main track, past a crowd that had mourned enough. All through that long day, nothing was heard but the barking of dogs and the breeze deep in the passageways.

The colonel who was at the head of the firing squad, could not forget that among those executed there was an old woman in black who told him his hands stank of blood. Returning home late in the night, he thought of his mistress' feet with their brick-red toenails, of the thumb she kept in her mouth, of the pills and the glass of water on the little cane table beside the bed. He rubbed his hands together, as if to avoid getting this smell of blood on her body scented with toilet water.

After endless hesitation, when he went into the room, he didn't see his fragment of dream on the bed. He didn't look at the majestic powder bowls in rosy glass, or at the perfume bottles, or at the chamber pot with the blue lotus flowers, or at the sewing machine, or even at the little chair. He ran out through the courtyard shaded by the shifting darkness of pale planets and heavenly depths, with that same flash of moon on his shoulder that used to go with him when, heart overflowing with love, he had sought out this great flower of beauty in the shadowy passages among the puddles and the lamplight. Scarcely had he emerged into the street when he heard a long sob in the sky. He looked up and saw his mistress in her dressing gown returning along the electric wires. "What are you doing up there?" he'd shouted. Awakened out of her sleepwalking trance, she dropped like a shooting star and crashed down onto the pavement.

She spent a whole week with compresses on her brow, weeping and suffering from nightmares in which she heard the braying of Breakback, the old donkey, in scenes of twilight blazing along the horizon of the last of the swamps, among the stumps of rose laurel and the great migration of doves, the whole world where poor people dwelt.

The days, the months, the years went like garments in free-fall down a whore's legs. They came to earth so slowly and so strongly resembling each other that signs needed to be traced in charcoal on the outside wall of the hut just beside the doorway, to name them. And there was beside the door at the height of a man a great profusion of spiky handwriting which signified the Cycle of Time and gave a regular pattern to human life. The first man who had this brilliant conception was said to have come into town with his machete, planted it in a pool of stinking mud over by the salt flats and announced to his astonished family:—Right here is where we build our house! He had driven away the mosquitoes and dried out this dirty porridge of earth full of vermin and assailed by tribes of gnats. The children brought sand from the nearby shore, the women water, the men stones. And the house had been built.

They named the days as they had baptised the passageways: after their own events. The simplest facts had great importance for them.

As each day had its special event, they had no problem finding names. And as the night also had its own, which had to be announced, there were night observers who walked around in the dark between the barely-finished shacks, watching out for the path the comets would take, listening for the direction the breeze came from and studying the position of the stars. To such good effect that they had almost established an astral system for town life (different from that of the lands of their origin limited to the cosmic lore of agriculture) able to predict the cataclysms of the drain overflow and of the long days of thirst and barking dogs.

The man who inspired most confidence in his star-gazing was called Cafenol Analgesic, because he had been the first to come into the ghetto with the chalk-coloured pills, which according to him had the power of putting to sleep anyone who suffered from headaches or migraine. In the beginning the people believed that Cafenol was in league with those who had come that time, now quite distant, when pills were given out to stop children being born. But later he came to be respected by all. He said that he would discover the mystery hidden between the stars and this unhappy world here below. He became a kind of sorcerer.

On one of his nights of contemplation, returning from the marshes, he saw a great light in front of the steps leading up to the verandah of Brother Ludovic, nicknamed Colic-of-the-Holy-Spirit. Believing it was a fallen star, he drew nearer and nearer and saw instead a shining horned beast sitting in front of the steps. Cafenol Analgesic cried out in such a loud voice that the people woke up and came out into the street and surrounded the shinning beast, who in a trice transformed itself into a stark-naked man, none other than the eldest son of the above mentioned Ludovic, whose wife, troubled by this great malediction, pushed her way through the crowd with a bowl of hot urine, and threw the liquid over the changeling to conjure away his evil spirit.

After this great shock, Cafenol Analgesic no longer pursued his contemplations, and the ordinary folk never discovered the astral secret of the unhappiness in this world here below.

That seemed almost to be a sign announcing calamities to come, for since that time the uprooted knew only misfortune, from the violent ravages of floods, to the arrival of those men who, with their terrifying machines, had constructed the walls of the big sheds.

The first day of August rose over Death's-Door; overcast, the colour of stardust. The first lights of the Feast of the Virgin appeared in a sad dawn over the ghetto, where there were no more branches of rose laurel decorating the old whitewashed walls, creeping over the corners of termite-eaten windows or twining at the threshold of doors trodden by the thousand-and-one bare feet of the great race of the dispossessed. For these people time has never changed. There is only a single endlessly long day: the day which saw them arriving with their bundle of woes, their saucepans and their children down the path beside the mosquito-creeks. Those who, by dint of mighty struggles, managed to own a shack, still remembered when almanacs had been given out, said to be the first of the year nineteen hundred and forty-three. They'd hung the calendar on a nail, and it was the same one which saw the great flood, the shadow of *Vivi*, the time when cattle and men were driven away from the gate of the big sheds, when the flag was run up the wooden mast of the yellow barracks, when Dinombien died. The thing hung up on its old nail still had its faded numbers, its cardboard yellow with age, all crowned by the picture of the President who, not long after, was driven out by striking students, shopkeepers, market higglers, after someone had hauled up to the top of the signal pole a miserable white flag which turned out to be a torn under-garment of the First Lady. The dawns and the dusks, the sun and the rains, the dust and the falling of stars occurred beyond hours and historical epochs, joining with the unending cycle of the Time of the Exodus and the great migrations.

Now, when John woke up that morning with the mint smell of his mistress' armpits still lingering on his lips, he shook her so violently that Passiona thought the hut was going to collapse with this earthquake. It was nothing but the frenzy of a man who wanted to say to his woman:
— Monday today. First day of the best month of you life! Even after she had emptied the piss out of the chamber pot into the gutter, she still hadn't made any sense out of this announcement, because nothing outside indicated the specialness of this Monday. The old drunkman was still haunting the corners of the huts. Babies were still bawling in the bleached-out dawn. And a pack of dogs was barking behind Walk-bout Woman who lately had taken to coming more often with her dangling-penis boy, as the wind of lazy dawns beat upon her. But when John took Passiona by the arm, slammed the door, told her why he'd come home very late in the night, and assured her it was time at last that each day had its colour, Passiona looked at her man's proud chest and said:—Djo, you dreaming. The days don't have a name no more. The months don't change.—They going change! he'd shouted, opening up the window which let the tune of the little boy's flute into the room. Furiously he pulled down from the old nail in the wall the almanac that dated from their first meeting, tore it right across and threw it out of the window. The bits of paper as the wind blew them away prophesied the return of the doves.—They'll come back, he said, those doves me boy love so much!
The night when, trembling with fear, Passiona watched John and Dorismé come into the little room with four other workers who sat on the old bed or stood near the lamp

casting gigantic moving shadows on the wall, it was the eighth of August. In low voices they talked all night and before dawn disappeared into the depths of the passageways, each in a different direction.

So, when the ninth dawn broke, it was Passiona who woke up first. She pushed the creaky old door open slowly so as not to wake up her man, stood in front of the gutter and for the first time smiled when she saw the old drunk-man, heard the children bawl and the pack of dogs barking in the distance. She looked up at the Pole Star, a tear sliding down her cheek:

— Tuesday today, she said.

The tenth day of August saw Passiona slipping in among the girls crowded outside a factory, pulling slips of paper out of her bodice, and calling to those who stretched out their hands or hesitated: "Jesus will set you free!" When they made out the contents of the paper, they didn't find verses of the Bible or the usual religious commentaries. Here was something about their own lives. "Jesus will set you free!" One girl threw away the paper. Passiona picked it up and offered it to her again:—Keep it in you blouse or under you petticoat, do not cast away the gospel of liberation proclaimed by Jesus from the Cross. Hands reached towards her all around. She hastened to take more paper out of her bodice:—Everywhere proclaim the word of Jesus! Go from place to place preaching the good tidings!

When the gate was opened and the girls disappeared into the factory, several of them turned round to look at this woman filled with burning zeal who went off down the passageways slipping the paper over doors and proclaiming under windows: "Jesus will set you free!" When she met Walk-bout Woman, she smiled to see that her bundle also carried the slogan "Jesus will set you free!" It was then that she realised John had spoken true about the eternal vagabond. She chased off the pack of dogs with an old stick and ran her hand affectionately over the boy's head. He said to

141

her with a sad little pout:

— I don't catch the moon as yet.

— The day not far off, Josi, when you going to pluck it for the happiness of the race, came the answer from the vagabond, to Passiona's astonishment.

The younger woman disappeared among the huts, calling, "Jesus will set you free!" She retraced the way old Dormelia had taken (I call your name, I can't call you from your path) when she was looking for the violent smell of the laundered trousers. She passed among the children all dirty in the dawn, stepped over the old car body where the hen was roosting, bucked with her left foot the can of Shell Company gasoline, passed by the outhouse with a door the Virgin's blue, lifted up the wire on which still hung some remnants of trouser munched by the pigs, released a panel of her dress that had hooked up on the barbed wire, crossed the ruins of the Plague-Wall, and stopped, dumbfounded, to see some fifty men coming up the avenue with placards raised and chanting in a warlike rhythm:—We demand our land!... We demand our land!

The human tide swept her on like a wave. These were country people, come to town to appeal for their land rights which were being refused by police in the rural militia, abetted by the lawyers.

— Our land!... We demand our land! The man marching with a white flag at the head of the crowd was the son of Brother Bienvenu, a hot-headed farmer who'd given his life to the peasant struggle.—They steal we land, woman. The land we work from father to son far back as we can know. That is all we have, that is our life, he said to Passiona who was now trapped in the crowd.—But you risk a heap of trouble making demonstration like this in the open street!—But we been already to the ministry that responsible. Them don't listen to what we say! You think those people got the right to tek we land as well? At that very moment a police siren screamed through the air, and a short time later a truckload of soldiers blocked the road against the peasants.—You are ordered to disperse! thundered a voice over a loud-speaker. Disperse yourselves!

— We demand our land!... We demand our land!

— You are ordered to disperse! Otherwise we shall be obliged....

— We demand our land! We demand our land!

Bienvenu held the flag high. Passiona was the only woman among these rough countrymen. She saw their undaunted looks and felt their courage. She shuddered deep inside herself and chanted with them: We demand our land! And it was just as she was catching hold of the flagstick to help Bienvenu lift it up that John saw her.

— What you doing here? he asked angrily when he reached her.

— Just what you see. These are brothers, poor like we. Me walk with them—We demand our land! She marched with Bienvenu towards the truck barring the avenue a few meters away.

— What a foolish thing you doing! These are not the comrades from *Incorrperaytid!*

— That too bad! she replied.

The troops had moved among the peasants and were thrusting them back with their rifles. The flag was torn from them by force. Passiona, who was still hanging on to it, took a blow from a gun-butt on her wrist. Though in pain, she hit the soldier who was trying to drag Bienvenu off to the truck. Disorganised, the peasants fled. Passiona took advantage of the confusion to direct the peasant leader away down a passage. With the demonstration scattered, the soldiers drove off at speed, leaving on the road the flag and Passiona's slip of paper, open for all to read: "Sister workers, proletarian brothers,...unity will make us free!" John caught up with them at the end of the passage:

— Let this man alone, I tell you, Passiona!

— Him is a brother, poor like we, Djo!

— You don't see what you did? You drop all your paper in the street!

— Mek them read them then. They can't kill the truth.

After nightfall, in the little room, the others watched Passiona come in, bringing the countryman Bienvenu. That long night punctuated by the barking of dogs and the sparkling of stars, John, Dorismé and their comrades came to see that Bienvenu was their brother. They clasped hands together in the lamplight and their breathing made the flame dance, casting light and shade over the walls.

Unfurling like a white flag, the eleventh day of August found the beautiful brown girl in such a state that the sun veiled over and rain fell from six in the morning until nightfall.

The night before, after the colonel had turned over for her pages of the heavy photograph album revealing nameless family members, sabres, medallions, epaulettes, boots, gold braid, parades on the garrison square or in front of the pergola decorated with the national colours, and after he had carried her to her royal bed among flowers, butterflies and the sublime chamber pot, she dreamt that she had woken up to the braying of Breakback. She took her father's machete and went into the darkness of the yard to the animal, which was tied with a rope to the old calabash tree. She struck the donkey with the machete until it was mangled flesh and bone. At the last machete blow she saw hundreds of fireflies settle on the heap of flesh. They came in such numbers that they completely obscured the corpse and their light only revealed the rope still tied to the calabash tree. Then she saw the donkey resurrected with thousands of stars in its body, mounted by a man with a shining lance— none other than the man who had bought Breakback in that little country market amid the smell of salt fish and the blue glow of indigo balls. In one bound the animal snapped the rope tied to the calabash tree, and like one of the horses of the apocalypse made for the dark fields and nearby corn patches with a scattering of stars and a warlike bray so piercing that it still echoed when she woke up to see the dismal rain and the colonel with his shirt-sleeves rolled up trying desperately to wrest the comb from her bleeding hand. It seemed to be welded to her palm. Each time he tried to tear it from her, she screamed so loudly that the whole house was shaken. She didn't want anyone to have the comb. Not even the colonel. The same man who washed his hands every morning in the bathroom basin before gazing upon his mistress' feet, beautiful as vigorous roots with their brick-red toenails.

They spent the whole dark day tussling, until the colonel, wretched at the idea that he couldn't take away this comb that made her fingers bleed, retired to the window. Just then he saw the garden shears lying in the courtyard in the rain.

— But they're going to get all rusty, he thought, and went out to pick them up.

When the beautiful brown girl saw him coming back with the shears, she feared he would cut off her hand to get the comb. So she leapt across the room, in a movement which smashed the sublime chamber pot, snatched up her little chair and dashed panic-stricken out of a side door into the rain. Running along the sidewalk, between the cars, bumping into people with umbrellas, slithering on the gleaming roadway, her hair down over her shoulders, the rivermaid was crossing the city.

As he came into the room, the colonel saw the broken pot. He searched the house, then he too dashed out into the rain. Heart beating and soaked through, he ran on. It was at the corner of the avenue that he caught sight of the pale silhouette of his mistress.—Come back! he shouted. Come back! You can't leave like that! Come back! His words were drowned in a gust of wind and rain which swept over the walls of the buildings and the tarmac of the avenue. He went on, transfigured by his mad passion. The beautiful brown girl then made her escape by signalling a *tap-tap* along the avenue. She got in quietly at the back and instead of sitting on the bench, sat on her little wicker chair. On that bus was written, ''The Lord shall fight for you, and ye shall hold your peace. Exodus 14:14''. *Our Lady of August* was still creaking along like a soul in torment through that world of water and rottenness.

She got off at the entrance to the ghetto, crossed the ruined Plague-Wall, went along the main track past the old fountain, Jesus-Grave, the miserable shacks, deeper and deeper into the passageways and there, where her poor parents' hut had been, was the huge surrounding wall of the big sheds.

When the colonel reached the entrance to the ghetto, he shuddered at the thought of going further: he thought he could see men lying in wait for him at every shack. He could hear the dogs barking and, with a heavy heart, retraced his steps towards the avenue, abandoning his pursuit of the beautiful brown girl.

And thus it was that on the twelfth day of August the news went around that the girl had come back with the rain. Brer Perceval told anyone who cared to hear that at last the time of doves and pink rose laurel had come again. The story of her return took on such a wealth of detail that the uprooted told each other that, after her flight, lightning had struck her fabulous room but had only broken the mirror of the polished mahogany wardrobe in which the dresses of cotton, taffeta and muslin, the transparent negligées, mosquito nets with butterflies and moons were impregnated with the musty scent of old relics; that in the midst of the mirror-splinters and the torn pieces of cloth a great bouquet had sprung up, opening over the mosaic floor; but that, at the colonel's lightest breath, like a sensitive Mimosa, it would close up tight.

On the fourteenth day of August, the colonel, broken-hearted at the loss of his love, delegated the search for the brown girl to his henchmen. They combed the shanties from the Plague-Wall to the edges of the most distant swamps, broke into the cottages of the Flower-Town quarter, flung out through the doors and windows cooking pots, jugs, chamber pots, chairs, plates, lamps and books, some yellowed with age or nibbled by the rats, others with pristine pages like the wings of doves.

When the colonel's men left the ghetto, disappointed by the results of their search occasioned by the unhappy love affair, women and children fell upon the papers fallen into the mud, intending to sell them to the secondhand dealers in the market. Then they heard Professor Belbonjour calling out as he came running towards them down the lane; they scattered and fled, not without carrying off a few torn pages. He saw there his books, his notebooks, envelopes and newspapers. Among them that scandalous headline ''Peace and Order reign in the slums'' on a front page already yellow with age, which he'd kept with some irony from the time when the woman had eaten her baby. Horror-stricken, he saw again for a few brief seconds his smashed glasses lying on the floor of a hot interrogation room:

— Where were you on Tuesday when the bomb exploded?

— I was at home preparing my classes.

— Do you know...? (His memory had lost the names on the list.)

— No.

— Did they visit your house two days before the Tuesday in question?

— I tell you I don't know anything about the people you mention.

— Where were you two days before?

— At home.

— What were you doing?

— I was with my sister.

— Where has she gone?

— Where I am right now, I'm not in a good position to answer you. I only know she's been kidnapped....

— Liar!

He didn't want to recall the moment when the heavy club came down, knocking him to the cement floor. There, before passing out, he had seen the powerful raised hands of the warder restrained by his interrogator. He shook his head as if to dispel these disturbing images, and bent down to pick up his things. There he heard the voice of a woman, who seemed to want to help him retrieve the papers from the mud, saying:

— The truth mek them mad, Professor.

Belbonjour looked at Passiona with an enquiring eye, wondering to himself who this poor woman could be who understood this insane violence. What truth was she referring to?

— Them is murderer, Professor, she went on. They kill Dinombien, they kill Raphael, they shot Dormelia and the man of Pedernales and so many more that struggling. You think we just lie down with all that sufferation? I hear bout you, how you do two years in jail and how you write book about this misery. Me husband Djo, he work in the big sheds. He tell me say, only unity can set we free.

Then Belbonjour recalled the woman handing out papers with her strange religious zeal.

— What in there (she tapped a finger on her forehead) make you write your books?—That plus this reality.—You know, my old Djo and me, we know how to sign we name and write a letter, but that is all. Yet we learn plenty things. We can't write big book, but if we could, people would talk plenty about this place.—You're more aware than I realised. But you know, I've learnt plenty too. I lost a sister that I loved dearly. And the days I spent in prison showed me the face of the fascists....—That is what?—Fascists, that's what you call them, people who're against freedom. I've been persecuted, but nothing can stop my feelings for the oppressed. Each time some violence comes I reproach myself for being cut off from the people. I was frightened, I saw people die and I was ashamed of myself. And yet, I went on writing...Look, I've begun a book on the situation which might show how....

Now Belbonjour had started reading his papers to John, Dorismé and Bienvenu. Passiona had arrived at the little house with the teacher, to be greeted by an embarrassed look from John, who pulled his woman aside and glared at her so fiercely she was afraid:—What is the problem, Djo?— Who is this man, Passiona? Is a fool thing you doing, him look like a judas.—Is a professor. He write books about poor people.

In his professional tone Belbonjour read out what he'd written, pausing now and again to explain a word. When he'd finished, Dorismé said:

— You don't know what go on in the big sheds. I spend a whole chunk of my life in there. Same way you don't know what the country like. Brother Bienvenu can tell you about that. Same way you don't say what we can do to get out of here, out of this poverty. A man of book-learning, Belbonjour, is no man for the struggle.

— You think my study leaves things out?

— That is what I know.

The professor took out a cigarette and Dorismé offered him a flame from an old lighter.

— What's your analysis?

— We not reading book, we getting our men together. The morning after we win, is then we need you, Belbonjour.

They hugged each other in a brotherly embrace. Then John clasped Passiona to him with the words,

— Tomorrow we going to overthrow the big men and they evil scientist!

— Them worse than that, replied Passiona. Them fascist!

Some said they'd seen her over by Death's-Door, with bloodstains on her dress, which was so white and transparent they were seized with shame and fear at the faint beauty of her breasts and the eternal modesty of her maidenhair. Others reported that, very timidly, they had come upon her washing her feet in the gutter water down Sorrow-Alley, as if she wanted to get rid of that strange dye which gave her toenails their unnatural colour. However, in spite of the small span of this world, locked into the indifference of moons, all the uprooted couldn't see her, though they longed to do so. They made do with luminous dreams through which she passed as if through great groves of rose laurels. So many stories were told about her that in the end the whole ghetto melted its sufferings into this dream which became an obsession that no one could do without—even Passiona, who met her on the thirteenth day of August, by Seven-Dagger-Cut, sitting in the little wicker chair. Early that morning, she was going up to this unhappy sister sheltering in an old doorway to give her a paper, when the sound of her footsteps woke the woman up. The sleeper raised her head and saw Passiona with her hand outstretched as if for the comb. She stood up in her marvellous beauty and disappeared down the passageway with the little chair, leaving Passiona to wet herself in terror.

152

John didn't believe a word of this until the evening of the same day when, coming back from meeting Bienvenu and Dorismé, he too met her by the little cemetery. Raising up the length of pipe which he carried at night to protect himself, he chased after the human form bending among the tombs:

— Eeh, you evil Vlingbinding! You not taking the bones of my son!

Then she turned, and John saw in a gleam of moonlight her white transparent dress, the faint beauty of her breasts and the little chair. He fell to such a quivering that from his suddenly stiffened rod he could feel something flowing which stuck to his thighs and made his knees tremble, just like when he made love to Passiona between a scent of mint and a loving word. The hollow sound of the pipe falling on a stone, the stars in the sky, the faint beauty of those breasts, the four legs of the little chair: when John stood firm again on his two feet all he could hear was a sob in the darkness.

That day the Holy Virgin Mary had left this earth. And the whole world watched, sad or uplifted, with tears or shouts of joy, the luminous train of trailing veils, crescent moons, fragments of stained glass, transfigured clouds of morning and showers of heavenly jewels amid the great vibration of organ music, the lofty totemic structures of the cathedral and the ecstatic setting of the Assumption.

Some dreamt of the brightness of her robe, or the light of her shrine, and however far away they were, they made up their bundles the night before, bringing in them ends of candles, sashes, royal blue handkerchiefs, also cut branches of rose laurel that wilted on the long walk. Others, who slept close by on the hard stone steps, were awake to hear the clack of wooden crutches on the flagstones or nervous scratchings of nails at the threshold of the closed main door; then they rolled themselves up again in their sad sheets, plaintive or mad, before being vigorously shaken, just before dawn, by the streetsweepers with their mournful litany.

The sweepers sprinkled water over the stones paving the square, to remove the dust and dirt so that they would shine like marble. They used old knives to scrape the melted candle wax from the sides of the crucifix, and with their brooms raised a cloud of dust which faded into the air or settled on the rose laurels. As dawn broke, garlands of coloured paper could be seen looping from one pylon to another and standing out against the pale blue of the sky.

When the first dove was seen at that early hour flying silently over the square, people thought that it must be the last one from the shanties which had lost itself in the darkness and now in the dawn light was heading for exile. But when more came, swooping in arabesques before flying off towards the rooftops, those who knew them made the sign of the cross and with much reciting of the rosary gave thanks to the Virgin. Mulatto girls came to the windows of old wooden balconies, rubbing their eyelids as if to dispel some dream, arranging a pot of flowers or combing their hair before a little broken mirror. It took the sound of linden wood fallen from a masons' scaffolding onto the cathedral steps to reveal another flight of doves who were nesting in the rose laurel boughs. It took the light of the last star in that silent morning to reveal, for the first time, that the sky was really blue.

Never once in the world of the shanties had anyone lifted his head to ask what colour it was, even Dinombien who couldn't bear the tears of his little boy at the gate of heaven. But they did know it gave great heat, and that, sometimes, it let fall upon the ghetto its ineffable shower of roses. That could be the only explanation for the sudden sublime blossoming from Sorrow-Alley to Death's-Door. On that morning, when they least expected it, the uprooted awakened to a display so magical that they couldn't remember ever having seen such an abundance of rose laurels except in the luminous dreams through which the brown girl floated with a glowing clip in her long siren's hair. It was difficult to push open the doors and the windows, to recognise the corner of a roof or the terrace of the brothel where the girls appeared in their robes so transparent, you felt perversity mix with desire, looking at the faint languor of their breasts, the curves of their hips or the soft golden down of their secret flower. That brunette, Anicia, the one just beside the flowering branches, looks so like Madeleine. These girls in their blossoming have never lifted their eyes to the sky. Perhaps to some languid *bolero* tune they've heard a voice singing *del cielo y de la luna*; perhaps after digging their nails into the ebony backside of a man who, as he came, muttered a few obscene words about shit and stars, they have murmured: *es un macho sentimental*. But they never looked at the sky and realised its purity until that morning when, hanging underwear on a bough, Anicia saw a dove fly up from the flowers.—Look! she said. They looked up and saw for the first time the blue colour of the firmament. Then peals of clear laughter rose up to follow the dove, like scattered raindrops. Perhaps they found this cloth of Mary too modest and were mocking her eternal virginity. The morning was so pure that even the girls carrying water were dazzled at the immense tabernacle spread before their eyes.

The fountain was covered with flowers, and they took a long time to find the twisted tap. It was those girls who saw emerging, in this sublime August morning, an old woman gnawed by time, all covered in dirt and tatter who dug her nails into the volcanic rock and cement of the fountain wall. The Wanderer appeared with such a fearful grinding of teeth and bones that the water-carriers realised at once that they were witnessing the mournful resurrection of the Old Hag, whose body had been crucified and left to rot on the top of Death's-Door. Sensing her own death coming, the Wanderer staggered from behind the wall with grimaces of pain and dragged herself down the main path through the girls threatening her with rockstones, pails and sticks. They made such a racket you could see doors suddenly thrown open, and out of the depths of the passageways came men who surrounded the Wanderer over by Jesus-Grave. There was a great stoning.

In a short time, all that was left of the Wanderer was a shapeless carcass lying in the dust, like the Bones of an ancient stellar Beast. There is no law against spitting on the remains of the Pestilence. See now! There it is! Didn't I tell you that one day the Beast would come out of its lair and men would tear out its eyes, the hairs of its skin, its nails and its teeth. Is so I tell you, not true?

So spoke Brer Perceval as he watched the crowd giving the death-blows and the children peeing on the vile bones with great shouts of laughter, accompanied by the ritual banging on pans.

This incident had scarcely come to an end when another tumult was heard to the west of the slum. When people went running in that direction, a human wave was seen forcing its way inside the big sheds. The great wave of poor people broke through the gate, strangled the watchman and invaded the big stone and cement yard. They had begun to vent their hatred and their revenge on these walls which they had seen advancing on their huts and their little plots of land, when a voice shouted in the middle of the yard. A worker, seen one night in Passiona's little room, stood on a table to address the crowd:

—Now that you taking back your birthright, your courage and your hope, don't destroy them. Don't break down the wall, don't break the machine! Is here we can work to feed we pickney, put clothes on we wife back, and build up we house. Plenty work here for all a we. It don't mek no sense to break down something made by we own hand on top of we own land. Is time now to put it to use! People time now!

From the quietened crowd came the answer in a vast thunder of voices: "People time now!" A young soldier who had rallied to their side raised his rifle in the air and shouted: "Power to the people!" And while the signboard of *Incorrperaytid* was being taken down from its place of honour, over by Cathedral Square the Virgin was ascending into heaven and the beautiful brown girl was sinking into the ground under the dusty laurels.

During the High Mass, there was such a milling about in the square that the worshippers went to the cathedral doors and saw on a mason's scaffolding, Dorismé, Passiona, Bienvenu and Belbonjour facing such an enormous crowd, it seemed as if the whole nation were listening to their words:

Our Truth is freedom. Our children are starving: we must find food. Our country is dying. Our country thirsts. We must sacrifice ourselves for its happiness. Our sacrifice is great. All those who sleep under this earth, the brave men of yesterday and of today, urge us on. Here is our freedom! Here is our power. Here, in this square!...

The crowd, uplifted, turned and saw the brown girl who moved through their dreams with the blood on her dress, and under it the faint beauty of her breasts and her maidenhair. She sat on a little wicker chair with something shining in her hair.

Our freedom and our power are there, under these boughs!

The legs of the beautiful brown girl could no longer be seen, nor could the feet of the little chair. She was sinking slowly into the ground, with the comb in her hair. At the sight of this vision the crowd drew back in terror. A wind blew over the square and through the quivering laurels.

You have been taught fear to stop you from claiming your own! You must not be afraid. What have you to fear? You are a thousand, they are ten! What have you to fear?

Only the head of the brown girl remained above the ground. Overcoming the panic inspired by this strange phenomenon, they pressed towards her as if to wrest her from those unknown powers which were burying her in the earth. All they could snatch back was the comb from the girl's hair. Then a wind like the end of the world blew up before the cathedral, sweeping away the crowd massed on its long flights of steps. The ground seemed to have hands, mouths, openings which parted and grew sensual to absorb this beauty. Eyelids almost closed, her hair becoming yellow leaves borne away in their autumn, for the last time something golden shining amid the multitude. The comb was shattered into a thousand pieces in the hands of the poor, workers, peasants, and great song of glory rose over the square, over the whole world of flowers and mounting dreams. Over the whole human celebration.

A thousand doves crossed the sky. And for the first time since the heroic days of the mosquito-hunters, the dispossessed saw falling on this land of stinking swamps and hovels, the unforgettable miraculous shower of roses. And so they came to understand the importance of those dates printed in red letters on the calendar.

June 1977—August 1978

ABOUT THE TRANSLATOR: Bridget Jones comes from North London and studied modern languages at Cambridge University, 1955-58. In 1963 she went to live in Jamaica with her engineer husband, and from 1964-1982 taught French at the University of the West Indies, Mona.

She has translated poetry by René Depestre and other Caribbean and African writers and has published a number of critical articles. A selection of her own poems appears in the Heinemann anthology *Jamaica Woman*.